C000125385

BEYOND THE MIST

BOOK 1 OF THE CHARA SERIES

Ben Zwycky

Published in 2015 by Sci Phi Publications
Edited by Lee Melling.
Copyright © Ben Zwycky.
Cover and internal artwork by Cat Leonard.
Originally published (in part) in *Sci Phi Journal*, edited by Jason Rennie.

The author asserts his moral right under the Copyright, Designs and Patents Act, 1988, to be identified as the author of this work.

All Rights reserved. No part of this publication may be reproduced, copied, stored in a retrieval system, or transmitted, in any form or by any means, without the prior written consent of the copyright holder, nor be otherwise circulated in any form of binding or cover other than that in which it is published and without a similar condition being imposed on the subsequent purchaser.

Contents

Acknowledgements

I would like to thank my wife and children for putting up with me and being an enthusiast first audience, and Jason Rennie for taking a big chance on me and buying the whole serial based on three chapters and a rough plot outline.

This story was originally published as a serial in Jason's excellent *Sci Phi Journal* alongside some talented new writers and established names that I never imagined seeing my own name alongside. The first three chapters appeared in Issue 2, with two chapters per issue after that, so spare a thought for those readers who had to wait two months per update!

I am grateful to *Sci Phi's* readers for the many encouraging words they had to say about my work, and for the very many good new friends I've made along the way.

Joanne Watson chose an excellent name for the protagonist, I hope you like what I've done with it, Joanne!

I am also indebted to John C. Wright, whose insightful philosophical essays inspired many aspects of this story.

Endorsements

"Like a science fictional Pilgrim's Progress."
D. G. D. Davidson, Sci-Fi Catholic

"A journey into strangeness...

A man with no name and no memories awakens flying in formless mists. So begins a strange journey in search of answers. Are we our memories or the result of our choices? How does one rise above the primitive? What is needed for civilization? Can we really leave the past behind and start anew? This is the journey where a man solves his greatest mystery: himself."
David Hallquist, author of "The Quantum Process".

"Sometimes you pick up a book and expect it to be one thing, and it turns out to be another. Pretty frequently that's a terrible experience ... Ben Zwycky's Beyond the Mist, on the other hand, fulfills its promise, even when its promise turns out to be different from what you expected ... All in all, Beyond the Mist is a great ride. It's gifted with a pace that never bores and seldom lags at all."
Joshua M. Young, author of "God Eaters"

Foreword

By John C. Wright

From the opening line, where the nameless narrator is passing through a mist, and does not know whether he is flying or falling, to the curtain line where he sums all he has learned in a single sentence, this is a book of strangeness and wonder.

The strangeness is the world in which the falling or flying protagonist is expected to discover: the wonder is in himself.

Old friends of the science fiction genre might recognize hints redolent of tales with a philosophical speculative bent. A WORLD OF NULL-A by A.E. van Vogt stars an amnesiac hero who discovers intrigue within intrigue against him; DEATHWORLD 2 by Harry Harrison is an unusually concise examination of the steps by which man departs from what Hobbes called the State of Nature and enters into civility and civilization; A VOYAGE TO ARCTURUS is a similarly concise examination of the steps by which a Gnostic soul, lost, tempted and tormented in a world of hostile illusions, fights its way back toward the ineffable glory that birthed it. From a genre older and more respectable than science fiction, PILGRIM'S PROGRESS by John Bunyan describes the obstructions presented to a Christian's soul fleeing the city of destruction seeking paradise, and he runs away from all he knew, ears plugged, crying out Life! Life! Eternal Life!

This book is unlike those, for it is its own creature, but, even so, the mystery of the journey of the falling man (or does he fly?) from the various temptations, traps, and dangers that threaten him, some physical and some more subtle, is the same mystery addressed in all these stories of how a lost man discovers himself.

For myself, I like books with likable protagonists, inventive, not easily deterred, whose efforts are ultimately rewarded, perhaps not in the way he first expected. How man discovers himself, defines his life, and names himself is an adventure all men share, and the mist of confusion (or is it freedom?) is one we all encounter. Enjoy.

Chapter 1 – The Mist

Am I falling or flying? I thought to myself as the endless mist rushed past my face, feeling the buffeting ripples up and down my skin but hearing nothing. *How long has it been – hours? Days? Months? Is this all there is?* I asked myself, unable to remember anything. *And who am I?*

A small plastic packet of water drifted past, travelling faster than I was, and I caught hold of it. A tube of some sort of food followed shortly afterwards.

Where do these come from? I silently asked as I consumed them, then allowed the empty wrappings to float away.

There was a faint light up ahead and I began to deliberately drift towards it.

"Away! Dive away! Avoid them at all costs!" a voice cried out behind me, and I leant away from it. "That is a ledge placed there by our cruel overlords. If you hit one of those, not only will it hurt you more than you can bear, but it will also rob you of your freedom. Seek refuge in the mist."

"A ledge? But what are they for?" I asked, turning to see who was speaking but could see no one, only a disturbance in the mist that indicated something was there.

"The overlords seek to lure us to our doom with promises of 'truth' and 'life'," the voice explained, spitting out those two words with disgust. "Do not listen to them, they only seek to hurt and enslave you. Here there is life, here there is freedom! Here they cannot touch us."

"Reach out for your life, find the truth and save yourself," a different voice called from the light as it came rapidly closer.

"Don't listen to him! Dive Away! Away! Don't let him reach you!" the first voice screamed as the light flashed past. "That was close – despicable creatures."

"So you know them?"

"I know *what* they are," the first voice replied, full of bitterness. "I have heard the stories, they speak of 'truth' and 'light', 'right and wrong', 'responsibility and self-control', it is nothing but lies to ensnare and enslave you. The mist is life, the mist is safety, here we fly! Here there is no failure or shame, duties or consequences, here we are kings!"

"How can there be lies if there is no truth?" the second voice called from a distance. I looked back to see a light approaching.

"It is one of them!" the first voice wailed. "Cover your ears, dive away! You will not enslave us!"

The second voice spoke with an authoritative calm as it gained on us. "To lie is to knowingly deny the truth. How can there be lies without a truth to be denied?"

"Stay away from us!" the first voice shouted.

The light was getting much closer now and the second voice no longer needed to be raised. "Do you not have eyes that were made to see? A mind that was made to think? Legs to stand on solid ground? A soul to make a difference? The mist is not life, the mist is a prison."

"A prison? Ha!" the first voice scoffed. "What do you know of freedom?"

The second voice seemed to grow in weight and vitality as it replied, "I know the freedom to stand and gaze at the beauty of creation, the freedom to love, the freedom to distinguish between right and wrong, the freedom to enjoy the fruits of my labour, know the satisfaction of a job well done and take the consequences of my actions, to find my context and live life to the full."

"Here there is life, and to more than the full!" the first voice said. "The freedom to create whatever reality you desire!"

"Any such creations are purely in your imagination," the second voice countered as the light came ever closer and split into two, revealing a human shape with lights attached to both shoulders. "You are merely playing in the mist, nothing real is produced."

"But that's the beauty of it!" the first voice enthused. "Total

9

control, none of it lasts any longer than you desire it to – as soon as it no longer interests you, it's gone."

"To be honest," I said, "that sounds more like a disadvantage than a selling point."

"Humph," the first voice snorted in disgust. "If you wish to enslave yourself to another man's reality, then be my guest."

It was then the second voice's turn to take on a slightly disapproving tone. "While you play these childish games and entertain yourselves to death, there is a vast world out there with beauty to discover, genuine adventures to be had and worthy struggles to take part in."

"How would I leave the mist if I wanted to?" I asked.

"In less than two minutes, we will approach a bridge across the entire chasm. I will provide you with a parachute to land safely on it and a light to help you find your way across, but this will be no easy journey."

"After all the risks I took to help you," the first voice accused, "all the ways I opened your eyes, you would willingly serve the overlords? Traitors like you make me sick, you are not worthy of my time."

"Then begone," the second voice said, "and let him make his choice."

"If slavery awaits me, and I am not convinced it does, then I prefer that to this empty swirl of contradictions – the chance to find my place, to touch something real and meaningful; it is worth the risk. Give me the parachute and light."

The first voice gave out a disgusted sigh and quickly drifted away.

"Here you are," the second voice announced, reaching out and grabbing my hand; it looped something over my arm and reached around to loop it over the other, then guided my hands to two halves of a large metal clip. "Attach the large clip across your chest, and then there are two smaller ones to attach around your thighs." I fumbled around with my hands until all three were snapped shut.

10

"The light is attached to one of your shoulder straps – I'm switching it on now."

A bright white glow lit up the mist rushing around me and I could see some of my own form for the first time. I seemed to be an adult human, though I was still a lot less visible than the human shape opposite me, whose clothing was much brighter and was wearing some sort of helmet.

"Next to your left breast is a handle that when pulled will release your parachute. That will slow you down abruptly, and then two handles will appear above you, one above each shoulder. Pull on the left one to turn left, and the right one to turn right. Are you ready?"

"Yes, I have the handle."

"Good. I will count from three and then you will pull. Three, two, one, pull!"

The straps around my thighs dug deep into my legs as the violent change in direction wrenched the air out of my lungs and tossed me around like a rag doll for a second or two, the flapping canopy lacerating the air around my ears. Gasping for breath, I looked up to see what appeared to be a network of glowing green veins in the mist a couple of metres above me, and two green ovals dancing close to my face. I grabbed at the ovals with each hand, assuming they were the handles, coughed and recovered my breath as the pain became bearable.

"Oh, that hurt."

Once the canopy was stable, I had the bizarre feeling of my body now having weight, and the background noise I had perceived as nothing was glaring in its absence. I looked down and saw the green glow of the illuminated man's parachute below me and to my left, with his two lights having now merged into one again with the distance.

"Now you are closer to flying than you have ever been in here. Practice turning left and right until you get the hang of it. Pulling both handles at once will swing you upwards and slow your forward speed – we will be doing that when we come in to land. Try it a little

11

now to get the idea, but not too much or you may lose all forward speed and begin falling out of control."

I tried several basic manoeuvres and began to grow in confidence.

"Look below us," called the voice from the light, "you will see a large orange light approaching. That is where the bridge is at its widest – aim to land at that point."

"Understood."

The mist made it difficult to judge how far I was from the orange light, which separated into a large glowing ring as I approached. Before I could judge how much to pull on both handles I hit the platform hard, pain shot up my left leg and I slid across the perforated metallic surface. My slide ended with me clinging to a very low rail with half of my body hanging over the precipice. I lay there motionless, panting and groaning as the other man made a much more controlled touchdown.

"Let go, you fool!" a voice called as its source fell past.

"Fly and be free!" another shouted.

"No more pain!" a third cried.

"Not the smoothest of landings," said my parachute provider, now standing over me. "If you wish to fall, then simply let go. If you wish to stand, say so and I will help you up."

"Help me, please, but my left leg, my ankle, it hurts."

I felt a pair of strong hands pull me carefully back from the edge, then the illuminated man methodically examined the injured limb. "A mild sprain, nothing more. Some discomfort, but with a little strapping you should be perfectly mobile."

I felt some sort of footwear and a layer of fabric removed from my injured joint, then the cool sensation of some sort of gel or liquid being applied, a length of elastic fabric wrapped tightly around the tender area and the footwear replaced. As this was being done, I caressed the perforated metal platform I was sat on, so solid and regular.

"There, now try to stand."

I made an attempt at standing, but fell back down before reaching a half-upright position.

"It may take some time for your sense of balance to adjust, and your muscles and bones may have lost some of their strength, depending on how long you have been here. With time and practice, that will all return," the illuminated man explained as he removed my parachute and hung the cylindrical light around my neck. I could see the glint of the metal floor for a few metres in every direction before the mist blurred all things into one. The parachute canopies were criss-crossed with rapidly fading fluorescent green lines, and he appeared to be stuffing the billowing silks into a hole in what I assumed was the centre of the platform.

After a brief buzzing, he retrieved each parachute as a small and compact bundle that he slotted back into its pack.

"They're now ready to reuse?"

"No, they are just compressed to make them easier to carry out of here. They will need to be refolded later." He took both parachutes over his shoulders, pressed something on the floor that switched off the ring of lights and stood to leave.

"The way out of here is narrow, but straight. Some walk their way out, some crawl, others give up and fall back into the mist – that choice is yours – but if you do make it out, then I will meet you on the other side," and with that he turned and walked away, his light and footsteps quickly fading to a vague background impression.

The mist seemed to close in on me, threatening to overwhelm my little white light as I sat there on the platform, alone and isolated. A distant voice screamed, "Away! Dive away!" as something fell past with a rush of air.

I watched the discernible ripples in the mist from the falling body quickly diminish to nothing, then attempted to stand again. After two more abortive efforts, I was finally able to rise and maintain my balance on two ponderous limbs. I stepped forward and back and from side to side to regain the feel of bipedal motion, and despite the polite protests from my left ankle, started to think that I could do this.

"Leave us alone, you monster!" another voice shouted as it's source fell past, and I sighed, looking down at the platform on which I stood and peering into the greyness in the direction the illuminated man had disappeared.

"I've made my choice," I thought aloud, and began slowly walking forwards.

Chapter 2 – The Walkway

After about five metres, the platform abruptly ended with the same low railing that was perhaps ten centimetres above the floor and much more reflective than the supporting surface, forming a clear delineation between solidity and void.

I must have misremembered the direction he went, I thought, then began sidestepping to the left, counting out loud as I went.

All I saw were identical slightly curved sections of railing. As I moved, I was struck by how rigid the floor beneath me was. There was no discernible bounce to it despite, I assumed, being a thin layer of material stretching across such a large empty space.

" … thirteen, fourteen, fifteen. Must be the other way," I thought aloud, retracing my steps as best I could, stepping twenty-three times to the right before finding a break in the railing. There a straight section less than a metre wide disappeared into the murkiness and a reflective arrow on the floor indicated this was the way to go.

"Well, that's fairly clear," I said to myself with half a smile, and set off on my way.

Soon the way back was just as murky as the way forward, the walkway I was on seemed to be narrowing little by little, and the spacious platform I had left behind grew ever more appealing in my memory.

Every so often there would be a faint rush of air as a body fell past without comment, though some hurled insults my way: "You're nothing but a slave!" … "What do you want from us?" … "Smash that despicable light!"

"But I'm one of you!" I protested. "I just want to see the real world! Don't you want to know what's out there?" I turned and leant over the edge to call after the rapidly disappearing voices, but in doing so overbalanced and found myself beginning to fall after them.

In a panic I flailed my arms about and managed to grab the railing, ending up dangling by one arm. After some effort I managed to secure my position by grabbing on with my other hand and then considered my predicament.

My fingers were starting to burn; the dead weight of my body was more than my arms were used to bearing. *This isn't fair; I was only trying to talk to them. I just overbalanced over the railing, it could happen to anyone. It's not my fault ...*

"Put out that light and join us," whispered a passing voice, sending shivers down my spine.

From my position and by the light of the lamp around my neck, I saw the underside of the walkway and the twin reinforcing I-beams underneath it that disappeared into the mist towards ... *something*.

"I've made my choice," I said through gritted teeth as I swung my right leg up and hooked it over the railing at the third attempt. I hung there for a few seconds and then summoned up all of my remaining strength to pull myself up and over the edge, back onto the walkway where I lay panting on my back, breaking into a laugh of sweet relief for I don't know how long.

I stood and resumed my journey with caution but new determination, ignoring the hysterical shrieks hurled my way every so often. "Traitor!" ... "Mindless drone!" ... "You won't take our freedom!"

"Is there a way out of here?" a new voice timidly asked as it approached.

I felt the rush of meeting a kindred spirit, dropped to my knees and grabbed the railing firmly to prevent myself from overbalancing as I shouted back, "Yes! Yes there is! Look for the man with two lights, he'll help you!"

"Where is he?" asked the disappearing voice.

"I don't know, but look out for him!" I shouted over the edge then knelt motionless and silent, but heard no reply. *Must be too far to hear me. What more can I do?* I gave a long sigh, then stood and continued on my journey.

A little while later, the railings began getting thicker and closer together, and a faint light ahead was becoming brighter and more distinct. Also, any falling sounds were only ever behind me.

"Must be getting close," I concluded, and pressed on. A few metres further on, there was a metal bar that joined the two railings, and then another, and another, giving the appearance of a ladder running along the ground.

Curious, I thought as I carefully stepped over the bars, but as I did, the walkway began sloping upwards, though I could see no joint or curvature in the floor or ladder. Another step forward and the slope was even sharper, causing me to stumble back, and the slope was immediately reduced again, though there was no visible or audible sign of the platform tipping or curving.

"What?" I exclaimed, and tested the phenomenon again, producing the same result of the entire walkway seeming to slope upwards as soon as I moved forwards, and levelling out as I moved back.

I looked to the side and behind me, there were no other branching paths or trapdoors in the floor, so I carried on, leaning further forwards as the slope continued to get steeper. I began placing my feet on the horizontal bars, climbing them like a ladder, which my left ankle didn't appreciate so much. This gave me the strange sensation of the slope being steeper by my head than it was at my feet, despite the ladder being straight, which I could now see more clearly as the mist thinned and the bright white light formed a sharp circle at what I presumed was the end of the ladder.

As the ladder reached near-verticality, the walkway floor ended and I could see conical walls narrowing towards the circular light, which seemed to be some sort of open hatchway. I continued to climb the now completely vertical ladder, but just before arriving at the hatchway I reached across and ran my fingers across the conical walls, finding their unyielding metallic coolness invigorating. A faintly acrid but not unpleasant fragrance was carried to me by fresh air drifting down from the opening, which was quite a contrast from the vague mugginess of the mist. Below me, I could see the end of the walkway hanging straight down from the hatchway and disappearing into the mist.

Intriguing, I thought, then climbed the final few rungs into the light.

Chapter 3 – The White Space

As my head came up through the hatchway, everything around me was white, the brightness hurt my eyes until they slowly adjusted and began picking out details- shapes and outlines in the walls, rectangular panels with rounded corners everywhere, a round sofa with several gaps in it encircled me, and my own form was clear. My hands, appearing mature yet still youthful, the dull dark green of my clothing, the strange dull grey straps around my torso –

"Well done," a familiar voice said. I turned and saw a man seated on the sofa dressed in a pure white jumpsuit, the only vibrant colour in the room being his lightly tanned face, dark brown hair and piercing blue eyes.

"The man with two lights?"

The man inclined his head and smiled. "Correct. Please take a seat." He indicated to the sofa opposite him. I climbed a few more rungs, then stepped across and slumped into the sofa, marvelling at its softness and the wrinkled texture of its upholstery, which came as sweet relief after all of my exertions. I closed my eyes for a moment and gave a soft sigh, then looked across at my guide, my mind full of uncertainty.

"Who am I?"

"Whoever you choose to be."

"Don't I have a name?"

"Not that I am aware of, no records are kept of who you were or how you came to be here. You are free to choose a name for yourself at any point, or remain nameless for the rest of your days. You have been given a fresh start, what you do with it is up to you."

"Do you have a name?"

"I do, but I cannot tell you since it may influence the name you choose for yourself."

"Can I call you something, like, Lightman?"

"Of course, whatever you wish."

"Lightman it is then," I said with half a smile, then gazed around the room again. "So what is this place?"

"The space between."

"Between what?"

"Between the Gravity Ring and what lies above it."

I looked up, my eyes following the ladder to the ceiling where it met a closed hatchway. "And what does lie above it?"

"That is for you to discover, should you choose to go there. I am not permitted to tell you about anything ahead of you, only to describe what you have left behind."

My gaze returned to Lightman. "So ... Gravity Ring, was it? What is that?"

"Much as the name implies, it is an underground ring of artificial gravity. It is designed so that once you are dropped into it, you keep falling indefinitely, never meeting a wall or other obstacle for as long as you choose to remain there."

"But what about the bridge across the chasm? Doesn't that count as an obstacle?"

"It is only extended when someone accepts the offer of escape from the ring, as you did."

"But what if someone collides with it? Wouldn't that kill them?"

Lightman gestured to the grey straps around my body "That harness you wear allows you to be subtly guided around it, and away from the walls, so no one comes to harm in that way. The mist allows those within the ring to imagine that there are no limits to where they can freely drift."

"If you have that much control, then why give me a parachute? Why not simply guide me to the exit?"

"To place you in control of your own destiny, and so you experience the consequences of your actions. If an easy life is what you desire, then step back down through the hatchway. Your nutritional needs will be met, you will be protected from physical harm, and you will not be required to perform any work. No responsibilities, no expectations, no consequences."

My eyes were drawn to the lower hatch and the greyness beyond it, and a sickly feeling rose in my stomach. I followed the ladder up to the upper hatchway again, intimidated by its opacity.

"And up that way is the real world?"

"Up that way there are no guarantees."

I stared into space for a few seconds, considering what horrors that could entail, then closed my eyes and took a deep breath. "I'll take it."

"Most commendable." Lightman tapped a pad in the armrest under his right hand, and the hatchway below us closed. "Your harness will be more of a hindrance than a help there, allow me to remove it." Lightman stood and stepped through a gap in the sofa, moving behind me and taking hold of something on my back.

Several taps later, a series of light clicks ran up and down my spine and a light tension around my chest and neck was released. The harness detached itself from my legs and shoulders and a whole new range of motion felt possible, transparent covers lifted from my eyes and retracted, widening my peripheral vision. Plugs came loose from my ears, and gentle white noise was replaced with a chorus of subtle background sounds, quiet hums and the occasional muffled click from behind the panels around me.

The new freedom of movement brought with it a new uncertainty as the posture support from my harness was now absent and I began to slouch, then attempted to sit upright. "This is going to take some getting used to," I muttered.

"I expect it won't be the last time you tell yourself that," Lightman said with half a smile. "How's the ankle?"

"Better, but still a little painful."

"All right, let's see what we can do about that." He moved around to the front of the sofa and tapped a panel, which caused a drawer to open next to my left foot. The drawer had a black cloth across the top of it with a slit down the middle. Lightman removed my shoe and ankle support, then placed my foot into the drawer. The

22

cloth tightened gently around my limb and was warm and silky to the touch.

I couldn't see what was beyond the cloth, but the bottom of the drawer felt soft. A warm sensation flowed through my ankle, then a faint breeze across the joint accompanied by a muted hiss seemed to melt away the remaining discomfort.

"That should do it. It'll still be a little weak for a while, but as long as you don't go in for any acrobatics in the near future, you'll be fine."

"Thank you. Wait, someone fell past me when I was on the walkway – he was trying to find a way out. I told him to look out for you."

"Another agent was sent to deal with him as soon as I closed the hatch."

"Another one? How many of you are there?"

"Enough to cope with demand. Now, let's prepare you for what lies ahead."

I took my ankle out of the drawer and looked down at the dark fabric. "How does this device work? Can I take a look inside?"

"Your inquisitiveness is admirable and will serve you well, but there is a good reason for the dark fabric. The radiation in this device is good for joints, but bad for eyes. If you value your eyesight, then please just take my word for it."

"All right. So what's next?"

"Now we get you dressed for the occasion," said Lightman, reapplying the ankle support, then stood and moved past me, placing his hand on a panel in the wall. The panel slid to the side, revealing a long white corridor.

"This way, I promise not to leave you behind this time."

"We're not going up that way?"

"We need to make room for the next adventurer, and equip you for the next stage. Where we're going has another ladder up."

I followed.

23

The corridor stretched on for about twenty metres or so, the same white panels coating the walls, floor and ceiling. It was hard to tell from this distance whether the corridor ended in a junction or a wall. Every other panel along each wall was labelled with some sort of alphanumeric code.

"How big is the Gravity Ring?"

"It has a major radius of three kilometres and minor radius of two hundred metres, if that helps you to visualise it," Lightman said with a grin.

Six times pi is just under nineteen. Given a normal terminal velocity... "So, about five minutes to complete a circuit?" *Wait, how did I know that?*

Lightman stopped and nodded, impressed. "Depending on your body position, between four and six minutes to return to where you started. Those content to remain in the mist are basically reducing themselves to eloquent goldfish."

The fifth panel on the left had a grey square in the middle of it. Lightman pressed his hand against the square and it turned white, then the panel slid sideways to reveal a narrow corridor.

"In here." Lightman beckoned and headed down it. I followed, unable to see past my guide. Ahead of us was a faint whirring sound and that of a panel sliding, both of which stopped before we reached the end of the corridor after three or four metres.

"Here we are."

The corridor opened out into a room that was a little under three metres square. In the far right corner was a ladder against the wall with a closed hatchway in the floor below and ceiling above. In the opposite corner was a simple chair, next to that a small shelf on which was a book and pair of hiking boots, above and beside that were two hooks on the wall. A large green rucksack hung on the one nearest the shelf, and on the next a green waterproof coat of some kind. There was a vaguely familiar and pleasing blend of scents in the room that I couldn't quite identify.

"Those simple shoes you are wearing will be no good to you up there; these will protect your feet and ankles on all types of terrain. The rucksack has all the supplies and equipment you will need, the manual instructs you in how to use them. Feel free to peruse it at your leisure here, but once you leave, you will need to seal it in its protective cover whenever not using it."

"Right." *Equipment? Terrain? Protective cover? What is up there, and what is that smell?*

"Do you have any questions?"

"Yes, what is the pleasant smell in here? It's somehow familiar."

"Aha." Lightman smiled and pointed to the upper hatch. "That is a whiff of the air from up there. Scents are powerful memory triggers. That you are familiar with it means you most likely already have some of the skills you will need. Hopefully that is from your previous life, and not that you were sent back to the Gravity Ring from the next stage."

"You can be sent back?"

"Yes, anyone found within the double ring of white markers after dark will be tranquilised, have their memory wiped and be dropped back into the Gravity Ring."

"Oh. What could happen to a man to make him want to go back down?"

"As I said, I am not permitted to tell you about the next stage. All I am permitted to say is that the passage for moving on from the next stage is adjacent to its lowest point. That passage is always open, anyone attempting to block it is also thrown back into the Gravity Ring."

Did I do that? Was I some sort of criminal? I shuddered at the thought. "Well, I'll do all I can to prevent that happening to me, um, again?"

"It is not the only possibility, and whatever happened in the past, whatever brought you to this point is irrelevant. What matters now are the choices that you make from this point on. Before I leave you, there is one last thing you need to know. That light around your neck also functions as an emergency signal. If you find yourself in serious danger, press the button quickly three times, and we will get you out of there."

I looked down at the light and gulped. "Um, understood."

"Good, I must leave you now. In your own time, peruse the manual, familiarise yourself with your equipment, dress yourself and head on up. The lower hatch is locked, and the upper one is open, but will lock itself behind you when you close it, so take everything with you on your way up. Good luck on your journey."

"Thank you."

I opened the first page of the manual and scanned down the contents page, glancing across at the rucksack and noting the various items. "Hmm, that's the tent, sleeping bag, canteen – the cooking utensils will be inside, I suppose."

I looked up at the hatchway, a gently pulsing dull green circle in its centre beckoning me upwards. I looked back down at the manual, but couldn't focus on it, my eyes were drawn back up to the circular portal to ... what? *What is up there?*

I could stand it no longer; I placed the book in a clear plastic sleeve on the back of the rucksack, changed my shoes, put on the coat and rucksack and climbed the short ladder. At the top, I reached up two trembling fingers, stopping two centimetres short of the light, then closed my eyes and withdrew my hand a fraction.

I took a deep breath and opened my eyes.

"I've made my choice."

I reached out my fingers and touched the circle. It turned bright green, and with a gentle hiss the hatch slowly opened.

Chapter 4 – The World Above

I gasped as the smell hit me. All manner of earthy, floral and arboreal scents graced my nose. There was a gentle buzzing of insects, distant birdsong and the rustling of leaves by a light breeze. I looked up at a blue sky dotted with puffy white clouds. Gold and purple butterflies fluttered overhead. I stepped up a rung and the sounds became clearer, all around I could see the tops of green trees, some covered with needles, others with broad leaves of various shapes and shades of green. Up another rung and my eyes moved above ground level. Lush green grass ahead of me, dotted with flowers of all shapes, sizes and colours: deep reds, yellows, blues, purples and everything in between; domes, cups, bells, fans and a great curtain of yellow and white stars that hung down from the nearest tree. Rough dirt tracks drifted off into the trees in three directions. To my left and right, further hatchways like my own spaced three or so metres apart protruded from the soil like metallic bubbles rising from the depths.

I clambered out and crawled across to the nearest patch of grass, stuck out my tongue and touched the green blades with it. They had a rough, minty taste to them. A little further and I inhaled deeply the intoxicating sweet fragrances of the flowers, making me slightly light-headed. I slipped one arm out of my rucksack and rolled onto my back, stared up at the slowly moving clouds and sighed.

"I was afraid of *this*?" I laughed.

I shielded the direct sunlight from my eyes with one hand so I could take a better look at the faint red crescent near the sun. From this position, the crescent appeared as big as the thumbnail of my outstretched hand.

"Red. Iron. Sidereos? I wonder where Leukos and Chloros are?" I said to myself, looking all around the sky for those other somehow familiar objects, but failing to find them.

I stood, hooked my rucksack back on and went over to one of the broad-leafed trees. Its bark was a greenish grey but covered in deep widened cracks whose colour progressed to a light brown the deeper you looked into the crack, as if a young new tree was slowly bursting out of an old hardened skin. The greenish bark was firm and rough, but ever so slightly spongy to the touch. One side of the trunk was carpeted with a bright green straggly growth that was soft and velvety, like a well-kept lawn.

I took a closer look at the leaves themselves: small and roughly oval in shape, on some branches they were a paler shade of green than on others. Each leaf had a set of fine branching lines across its surface that was a little lighter than the bulk of the leaf. I moved my head around to see if the other side looked any different, and the lines were much brighter and more visible. I could see that those branching lines themselves branched out even finer, as did the branches of the branches, and their branches … I assume they went on branching far beyond by eyes' ability to distinguish.

So intricate, I thought. *I guess I wasn't a botanist, since I have no idea what any of these things are.*

My eyes moved past the leaf to see back the way I had come. The ground I was on sloped quite gently up to the metallic bubbles, then grew steadily steeper and steeper, culminating in a perhaps sixty-metre vertical cliff-face that gently curved around to my left and right as far as I could see before the trees blocked my view.

Looks like I'm in some sort of bowl, which would make the lowest point that way. I pointed a finger back over my shoulder. *Though it wouldn't hurt to stick around and explore this place a little more …*

I turned and joined the middle of the three dirt tracks into the trees, ducking past a cloud of swarming insects revealed by a shaft of light. I noticed one had landed on my hand and I brought it up to eye level to take a look. Its tiny translucent wings and spindly legs seemed almost comically oversized for its tiny round body and head, with the long mouth that was reaching down to my skin …

Oh, we don't want that. I quickly brushed it off, noticing a small white blotch on the skin where it had been. *That's probably not good, I should check the manual for what to do about that.*

I put some distance between myself and the cloud of insects, then noticed a tree ahead of me that was unlike the others in almost every way. It had a bulbous 'trunk' that was a mottled purple at the top, various blotchy shades of blue at the bottom, and in between was roughly vertical stripes of light and dark purple with the occasional group of dark blue patches. A network of branches carrying large broad spiky green leaves spread from the top of the trunk, some of those branches hanging down under the weight of fist-sized globular clusters of bright yellow fruit.

I moved closer and picked one of the fruit. It was egg-shaped and about a third of the length of my little finger. Its skin was smooth and soft, yet firm. I sniffed it then took a bite; it crunched between my teeth and tasted sweet yet tangy, like a pear mixed with honey and lemon.

Very nice. I nodded to myself, and went to pick some more fruit, then noticed a human silhouette on the trunk. Seeing my own shadow to my left, my pulse quickened and I turned to the right.

Nothing but the trees I had just come from.

I looked all around for the source of this other shadow, or anything out of the ordinary – as much as I could tell. I didn't find anything, which was both a relief and a disappointment.

I glanced back at the tree trunk to see that the silhouette was still there, but on closer inspection, it clearly wasn't a shadow. Its outline was human-shaped and a little blurred, but its colour was wrong: a little darker than the light stripes it replaced on the tree, but much lighter than the dark ones. Besides that, the head was much darker than the rest of the shape, a dark blue contrasting with the light purple of the body. As I stood there looking at it, the blurring around the edges of the body and head shape faded away, though it was still far from sharp.

I wonder ... I glanced to the side to check no one had reappeared, then slowly lifted my right arm and held it there.

The arm of the silhouette faded away and an upraised arm slowly appeared.

So this is my silhouette?

I held both arms out to my sides, and the silhouette again gradually shifted to match my form five seconds later.

This plant is copying me. Is it trying to communicate?

"Hello, Mr Tree. Can you hear me as well?" I waved both arms up and down, and soon the arms of my silhouette became blurry transparent wings against the trunk's original stripes, but there was no discernible response to my voice.

"Mr Tree? I hope you don't mind me taking some more of your fruit. My compliments to the chef, by the way."

I moved my hand back up to the nearest cluster of yellow fruit, then noticed its position was opposite one of the blue blobs on the trunk, the other blue blobs being also opposite a cluster of yellow fruit.

"Wait a minute, yellow ... blue. Green ... purple, that's just the opposite colour. Those stripes, are the tree trunks all around; it's like a rough photo negative of its surroundings."

I leant in and saw the tree's bark was covered in little half-centimetre circular indentations, each one slowly reacting to the light that hit it. I touched one of the indentations with the tip of my finger, it was covered with some sort of sticky sap and came off the tree very easily. Once detached from the tree, it was a translucent inert cylinder with rounded corners. The hole it left behind continued to react to the light and appeared to contain another smaller version of the 'lens' deeper within the hole.

"What is this, a seed? Oh, I suppose this colour display is to draw you in to touch the seeds, which then stick to you so you spread them. Very ingenious, Mr Tree. I tip my hat—"

I stopped myself just before my sap-covered fingers reached my forehead. "That would make a good first impression, walking around with my hand stuck to my head. Anyway," I said, reaching for a cluster of fruit and disconnecting it from the branch. "As an expression of my thanks, I'll be sure to plant this seed in a nice spot somewhere. Was a pleasure doing business with you."

I put the cluster down on a clean-looking patch of fallen leaves and used my non-sticky hand together with my other elbow to make a suitable space in my rucksack for my little haul, adding a second cluster to the gap, then scraped the sticky seed into my coat pocket, wiping my hands on fallen leaves to remove as much sap as possible.

I stood and faced the tree again, moving from side to side and waving my arms in various ways, watching the various transparent blurry shapes I could produce.

"Woo, I'm a ghost." I laughed. "I should do this with ..."

My smile faded.

Who? Do I have any friends? Is there someone waiting for me at the end of, whatever this is?

I sighed, put my pack back on and trudged down the track, then noticed a little blue bird flitting from treetop to treetop overhead. I watched its carefree lightness, skilful precision and the apparent joy in its song, then imagined myself soaring and swooping, banking and gliding high up above the ground, taking in all the sights and going wherever I wanted. My mood suitably lifted, I reached a marshy expanse in which large flat stones had been laid to continue the path and skipped from one stone to the next, humming a barely remembered tune to myself.

I stopped by a upright white stone about half a metre high. There were other such stones dotted in among the trees forming a gently curving line. Ahead of me the ground began to slope upwards and there seemed to be another such line about twenty metres further ahead, where the trees ended. Beyond that, I could see nothing but sky.

This must be the double ring of markers, so let's see what's beyond that.

In amongst the rustling of leaves in the trees overhead, a subtle noise caught my ear as I approached the crest …

Is that laughter?

Chapter 5 – The Waterfall

"Wow."

I stepped between the last two trees and the whole valley opened up before me, maybe six kilometres wide and thirty long, shaped like a staircase of successive half-bowls. In front of me was the crest of one of those bowls, the start of a steep but shallowing slope covered in fan-shaped plants, each looking like a set of green ribbons had been wafting in an updraft then froze in place, though they still rocked gently back and forth in the breeze.

In the distance beyond the bushes, clumps of trees dotted the grassy plain, followed by more substantial woods and rock formations, while down the middle of it all snaked a wide silvery river.

The sound I had taken for laughter was the gentle babble of a small stream echoing up a rock chimney that ended just below my feet, the chimney itself being five or six metres deep. The stream tumbled down the slope and veered off to the right until it joined the river a kilometre or so away. The breeze dropped and with it the rustling of leaves overhead, unmasking the distant sound of rushing water down and to my right. I stepped around the chimney onto a rocky outcrop and followed the noise, discovering that perhaps five hundred metres to my right and fifty below me, the river split into a number of small waterfalls feeding a large oval pool of crystal clear water, about fifty metres long and thirty wide.

Most intriguing of all, there seemed to be someone swimming in it.

The path down to the pool meandered across the slope, doubling back on itself twice. I approached the first turn at the top of a cliff, twenty metres above the pool, and could see that there were four waterfalls that fanned out from the exit to a narrow gorge possibly forty metres deep, its rock walls covered with moss and straggling vegetation, a faint rainbow shard hanging in the low cloud of mist that the waterfalls created.

Have I been here before? Is it always this striking?

On reaching the turn, I crouched down behind the last fan-shaped bush before the cliff's edge. Its fronds were smooth and undulating with a lens-shaped cross section that gave them rigidity. Despite the dull and soothing aroma that they gave off, my heart was racing as I peered through the fronds at the individual in the water, who appeared to be a young woman wearing very little, if anything.

What am I, a Peeping Tom?

I backed away from the bush, then began walking the rest of the way down the path, standing upright and looking straight ahead to give the woman I had spied on every chance to see me coming and get away if she so desired. As the path turned again and I faced the pool, I could see that she had caught sight of me and was swimming in my direction. I followed the track through the tall grass and reeds, ending at a large flat rock at the edge of the pool, its dry surface only five or so centimetres above the level of the water.

"Hello there," she called above the faint rumble of the waterfalls. "Come for a swim?"

"I was considering it."

"Then come on in, it's very refreshing, and a lot more fun with some company," she said with a slightly tired smile. "Your things should be safe and dry on there." She pointed at a large rock next to the one I was standing on, Maybe a metre higher and surrounded by bushes. It looked to be a good spot.

I turned back to her as she approached and took a closer look. She appeared to be in her late thirties and in good physical shape, with long brown hair, a long face with an elegant straight nose and the first hints of some lines on her forehead and under her pale blue eyes. It was also apparent that she wasn't wearing any clothes. She seemed to sense my embarrassment and smiled at me, which made things both better and worse. "So you're new here?"

"Yes, I got out of the Gravity Ring about half an hour ago, I think. This is a wonderful place."

"It is, and you haven't seen the half of it yet." She drifted to the flat rock I was standing on and rested her elbows on it, now less than two metres from me, the water droplets on her bare shoulders glistening in the sun, highlighting the smoothness of her skin.

I swallowed. "How, how many people are there here?"

"Hundreds – if not thousands. I'm sure you'll meet plenty of them soon enough. In the meantime, though ..." she traced little circles on the rock with a wet finger, leant her head to one side and looked up at me with a suggestive smile.

My stomach churned as I glanced across to the higher rock, then back at her, noticing a dark blue circle with a line coming out of it painted on the side of her neck.

"What's that on your neck?"

"A delicious little apple. If you want a taste, you'll have to get wet." She laughed and pushed away from the rock, treading water about two metres from the edge.

"Are you like this with all the men that come by?"

"Just the attractive ones." She smiled and playfully splashed some water at me.

I dodged the liquid projectiles with a smile, felt a surge of pride and took a step forwards. "How many has that been?"

"Does it matter?" she said with a nonchalance that struck me cold.

My smile faded and pride turned to revulsion as I pictured a long series of irrelevant men in her lustful embrace. "Yes, I think it does."

"Do you have a name?"

"No," I admitted, looking away.

"Then what's the harm? Two nameless bodies enjoying each other, who's going to mind?"

I looked back at her and the whole situation seemed suddenly false. "Is that all? I mean, is that all you want to be? A nameless shell for pleasuring every likeable man that comes along?" I gestured to the trees and waterfall. "Surrounded by all of this beauty, all of this abundance, and that's your goal in life?" I looked back up at the line of white stones at the top of the hill. "I had a name." I tried to peer back through the clouds of uncertainty, then shook my head. "I'll get it back one day. But nameless or not, I'll know. I can't hide from myself." I looked up at the sky. "Besides, how do you know we aren't being watched?"

She scowled at me. "Just who do you think you are, coming here and insulting me like that? You have no idea how things work around here." She turned and swam away back towards a pile of clothes on the far side of the pool. "Besides," she turned back towards me with a vindictive grin as someone jumped me from behind and pinned my arms to my sides, "I never said we weren't being watched."

I struggled, but two other people emerged from the bushes and pinned me down to the ground, removing the light from around my neck and throwing it beyond the pool into where the river picked up speed. It landed in the rushing water with a barely discernible plop, as if disappearing to another world.

37

They then released me and allowed me to stand. All three had dark green clothes painted with light brown stripes. Their faces were painted with dark brown stripes and a dark blue apple symbol at the back of one cheek.

"Sorry we had to do that to you," said the one who had grabbed me from behind, "but we had to be sure you wouldn't panic and activate your beacon."

"Why?"

"Because anyone who does is thrown back in the Gravity Ring."

Chapter 6 – The Apple Tribe

I stood there dumbfounded for a second, then glanced at where the beacon hit the water. "It sends you back to the Gravity Ring? Wha – how do you know that?"

"Because every time we've seen someone activate their beacon, they disappear and we either never see them again, or a few days or weeks later they come back from that part of the valley with no memory of us, just like when someone gets badly injured or sick."

"When people are hurt or sick they disappear?"

"Come with us to our camp, we'll explain on the way."

The three of them led me around the edge of the pool under the cliff to a cave entrance masked by reeds and vines. I was taken aback by the change from the light and warmth of the outside to the cool near darkness of the cave, together with the sudden drop in background noise to be replaced by eerie echoes of dripping water and muffled ghosts of the world outside. We stepped around a shallow puddle as our eyes adjusted to the gloom.

"It's not as if you disappear if you scratch yourself; it's only a really serious fall or being stabbed or clubbed that makes it happen."

I drew a nervous breath. "Does that happen often?"

"Only if you get into a fight with one of the other tribes. Don't worry, you're one of us now, we'll back you up."

The tension in my shoulders eased. *Well at least there's that – wait, what am I getting into?*

We moved past a small hole in the wall to our left that let a shaft of sunlight into the cave, together with the muted sound of the waterfalls. The light illuminated a cluster of stalactites that reached halfway down from the ceiling, a trickle of water danced down them into a deep half-metre channel across the whole of the floor. We stepped over the channel and continued down the tunnel, where there was just enough light reflected off the stalactite to see where we were stepping, helped by another hint of daylight up ahead.

"So is there a sound or something when it happens? I mean the disappearing."

"No, nothing. With the beacon it flashes a bright blue light just before they disappear, but with a fall or fight, they just hit the ground and a second or two later, they're gone."

"And you don't find that, disturbing?"

"You get used to it – it's just the way things are."

"I suppose so." I couldn't help but find the idea extremely disquieting. *Did that happen to me?* I imagined being impaled with a spear and shuddered, instinctively putting a hand to my stomach.

I tried to shake off the thought. "So how many tribes are there?"

"Well, there's the Apples, the Pears, the Plums, the Peaches and the Cherries; beyond that there are some other tribes who live on the rocks that we don't have any contact with, maybe some other groups we don't even know about. It's a big place."

"They're all named after fruit?"

"After the fruit trees they have control over."

"So you guys are the Apples, then?"

"Yep."

We reached the end of the tunnel, which emerged among some trees on the other side of the pond, and standing there were three women who had wrapped themselves in sleeping bags, covering everything from the neck down. On the left stood the woman who invited me into the water, who was giving me a venomous glare; the other two were a little more youthful and appeared to be thoroughly amused at her annoyance. The one in the middle had a tanned complexion, high cheekbones, a hint of curls in her shoulder-length black hair, a slightly upturned nose and strikingly dark brown eyes. The one on the right had long auburn hair, a rounder face with freckles, a snub nose, a narrow mouth and sparkling green eyes.

"And these are our three chief recruiters. Behold, the Unhookable Man!" The three men cheered and the older woman switched her glare to focus on them.

"Ooh, fear Queenie's wrath!" My guide laughed, throwing up his hands, then smirked at her. "Losing your touch, aren't you?"

There was a flash of fear in Queenie's eyes before her fire returned, and my opinion of her changed. "Queenie, I'm sorry if I caused you any trouble … I mean, I didn't—"

My attempt at an apology was interrupted by Queenie giving me a sharp slap in the face. "That's enough of that. I'll be taking the next one and showing you all how it's done."

"Oh, come on, Queenie, we're just having a bit of fun."

"Hmph." Queenie turned away to face the pool.

"So, Hookless," said the woman in the middle, playing with the zipper on her sleeping bag and looking over her shoulder at me with a mischievous smile. "Do you think *I* could tempt you into the water?"

I must have blushed, because a raucous laughter erupted among the men.

"Hookless, that's a good one!" My guide punched me in the shoulder. "Come on, then, Hookless, up this way. I'll take your bag."

"Oh, right, thank you," I mumbled, rubbing my face and unhooking my arms from the heavy load.

We moved up the hill on the other side of the river, following a similar winding path. A two-row wall of large white plastic boxes, each about a metre long and half-metre high and wide, was laid along the top of the slope, with men armed with spears standing behind it.

"So, do those recruiters actually let men catch them?"

"Not if we can help it. We usually stop them before they get in the water; it's all about getting them to put the beacon down so we can throw it away. Sometimes our girl will have to draw them over to the other side of the pool, and we catch them there. On the very rare occasions that someone gets aggressive, we make him disappear to be on the safe side, but once their clothes are off people usually don't put up a fight. We have to look after our girls so they stay pretty. We have a lot of men guarding the whole area, controlling that pool makes a huge difference to our recruiting effort."

So not quite as bad as it looked, but still...

"Now that you've given me a name, do any of you have them?"

"Oh, right, I'm Natter, you've met Queenie, Teaser showed you why she's called that," Natter said with a grin.

"Yes," I said, looking down at the ground.

"The quiet one was Cat, this is Clam and Root."

I exchanged nods with my two silent travelling companions.

"So where do those boxes come from?"

"They get dropped overnight. I say dropped, they appear in various places before sunrise each day, containing basic food supplies. We have to fight off the other tribes to find them first. Once they're empty, we use them for a lot of things, those we filled with earth to fortify our slope."

"That is a lot of boxes, how long have you been collecting them?"

"Longer than any of us can remember. Years, decades?"

Up where the path ended there was a rudimentary gate made of branches lashed together with tent guide rope, which was open but guarded by a small crowd of people. Through the gate muddy trails wandered off in various directions, the largest of them leading to a great wood of apple trees. There was a vague odour of mud and sweat that tempered my enjoyment of the approaching sweet fragrance of apple blossoms.

On passing through, an older woman carrying a small metal pot stepped towards us, stirring the contents of the pot with her index finger and smiling warmly.

"Hello, Natter. Who do we have here?"

"Mama, this is Hookless. He resisted Queenie's charms," Natter boasted, giving me a pat on the back.

"Did he now? That's a clever boy."

"This is your mother?"

Natter smiled. "She's Mama to everyone."

43

Mama's eyes sparkled and her nose crinkled. "I like to look after my boys and girls." She drew her fingertip out of the pot, dripping with a purple liquid and reached towards my face.

I drew my head back. "What's that?"

"Don't worry, it's just blueberries." She traced a little apple on the back of my left cheek, blew it dry then kissed the top of my head. "There we go, welcome to the family." It was a simple gesture, yet given with a reassuring warmth.

"Um, thank you, Mama."

Natter nodded. "Let's take you to see the Chief."

We followed the widest trail, where loose stones had been trampled into the ground to make it a little less muddy. I became aware of a rotten smell ahead of us as we approached the woods, and an even more unpleasant stench coming from my left.

There were tents put up all around the woods, most of them either coated or heavily spattered with mud, and rows of the plastic boxes on either side of the trail. None of them had lids and they were filled with apples, there were also several stacks of empty ones beside them. Some of the boxes contained apples that were shrivelled and rotten, and hundreds of similarly decaying fruit lay under the trees among the fallen leaves. Straggly low bushes bordered the path on either side, meandering around the trees.

We continued along the trail through to where the trees opened up, just before the ground became steep. In the middle of the slope was a flat rocky outcrop in front of the entrance to a cave. The outcrop itself was maybe four metres above the ground at the lower end of the slope and less than two above it at the higher end. A tiny waterfall fell from the cliff-top, its spray landing about ten metres to the left of the cave entrance; a couple of tents had been cut open and turned into a tall screen around the point where the water hit the ground. A small stream flowed out under the screen, past the bottom of the outcrop and off to my right towards the river. An enormous bear of a man, at least two metres tall, stepped out of the cave onto the outcrop.

Natter lifted his head and puffed out his chest. "Greetings, Chief. Here is today's first recruit."

"Very good, Natter," the chief said with a deep growl that made me think he could break me in two without a second thought. "Prepare him for war, and do the same with the others."

War? I glanced across to Natter, who seemed entirely unsurprised by this order, so I did my best to appear similarly unflustered.

"Yes, Chief." Natter bowed his head, and placed my bag by the stream at the foot of the outcrop, next to another row of empty boxes. I was about to ask why, then glanced up at the chief and thought better of it.

Natter took me up another wide muddy trail around the trees.

"You're at war?"

"With the other tribes. Been going on for a long time, but the end is in sight now, now that we've had control of the pool for a few weeks."

"The pool is that important?"

"Oh, yes. Almost everyone coming out of the Gravity Ring is drawn to it, so we get far more new recruits than any other tribe."

"And what are you fighting over, if you get regular food drops?"

"Territory, and fruit supplies."

"Fruit?"

"Take a bite of our apples, or any of their fruit, and tell me they're not worth fighting for." Natter smiled, then his smile faded. "The food in the boxes is very basic, and each tribe keeps the harvest from its fruit trees for itself."

"But you have far more apples than you can eat, I've seen hundreds if not thousands of rotten apples all over the place, why don't you trade with the other tribes?"

"The last time that was tried, the convoy was ambushed and everyone in it disappeared. The only way to get everything to everyone is for us to take control of the other tribes. As I said, we're making a lot of progress in that regard, we were virtually unopposed

45

this morning by the Plums or Pears; we were able to collect all the boxes in the plains on either side of the river without so much as a fight, and they haven't tried to contest our control of the pool for quite a while now."

We came to a piece of open ground dotted with broken branches, stones and very battered trees that had been cut back to the rough size and shape of a man. Natter handed me a fist-sized rock and stood me about ten metres from the nearest target.

"There, see if you can hit it."

My first throw landed at the foot of the tree.

"No, no, put your back and your hip into it, like this."

After mastering rock-throwing, I was then instructed in fighting with a spear and shield, the spear being the knife from a survival kit tied to a sturdy branch with a piece of guide rope from a tent, and the shield being a lid from one of the plastic boxes with tent pegs and bits of wood jammed into the handle's hinge to keep it rigid.

By this time ten or twenty other new recruits had arrived and we practised hand to hand combat in pairs, using bare branches in place of the spears and short sticks instead of knives.

"In battle you will have both a spear and a knife. If your spear breaks or gets trapped, don't hesitate to drop it, draw your knife and move in closer.

"As you may have heard on the way here, we are winning this war, resistance from the Plum tribe and Pear tribe has dropped dramatically in the last couple of days. They know they're beaten; any resistance they put up now is just prolonging the struggle, increasing everyone's misery. Two or three more major raids, starting tomorrow, and this war will be over. Show them no mercy, never retreat and never surrender. If you see you're about to be surrounded, keep hacking away to take as many of those bastards with you as you can."

I stopped what I was doing. "You want us to die in battle?"

"Don't worry about being killed. You'll just disappear, be healed up and put back in the Gravity Ring. Thanks to our control of the pool, when you get out we'll recruit and retrain you again, together with all the people you killed."

That's actually quite brilliant, yet somehow very wrong.

"To that end, before we go out on a raid, we dip the blades of our spears in the latrine." Natter gestured in the direction of a cluster of tents in the distance, which was clearly where the foul smell was coming from. "That way even if you don't make your enemy disappear straight away, he'll get sick and disappear later."

I glanced at my spear and gulped. *Now that is just extremely wrong.*

My shoulders were now very sore and the insect bites on my hands and neck were starting to itch.

"That's enough for today, Hookless. Go get some food and rest. Clam will take you to your tent."

"Is there anything I can do about these insect bites?"

"Oh, you should have said, just put a little billow bush juice on it."

"Billow bush?"

"That fan-shaped bush with the wavy green fronds that grows near the river. Slice it into small pieces and squeeze out the juice. You can drink it, best diluted, but our recruiters rub it in their hair and skin to keep them pretty. It also helps with the itches."

"Oh, thanks."

"No problem—" Natter looked over my shoulder, started, then grabbed his spear and rushed past me. "Everyone grab spears and stones and follow me."

I turned to look in the direction Natter was going and saw a man in a white suit similar to the one Lightman wore. He was picking his way through the trees, carrying a small plastic container and examining the ground. I hurried after Natter without a weapon in hand.

"Get out!" shouted Natter. "You're not welcome here!"

"I'm just checking for poisonous plants growing here in your woods," the man called back.

"Wouldn't want everyone to get poisoned and stop the war, would you?" called Natter, breaking into a run.

"No, and we don't–"

"We'll give you war! Everyone attack!"

The man in the white suit ducked behind the nearest tree as a hail of stones and spears was hurled in his direction. As I rushed in to try and stop this madness, I noticed him reach for and activate the beacon around his neck, which emitted a bright blue light just before he disappeared from view.

When I arrived at the tree, where quite a crowd had already gathered, there was no sign of him. There was a bloodstain on the tree trunk and on the fallen leaves, and a lot of broken twigs on the ground. I looked up and saw a gap where I assumed many of the broken twigs had come from. I noticed a few were still hanging on by a thin strip of bark, some of those broken sections leaning against higher branches, and a bloody handprint on the underside of one of the thicker branches at the edge of the gap.

Those branches were broken upwards, so he must have gone up through them. But what about the blood stains? I don't remember seeing him get hit, the fight must have carried on after the beacon lit up, at least for a little while. Then he was taken up, and what, our memories were wiped?

"What's going on, Natter? The guys in the white suits are the same people that drop the boxes of food, aren't they?"

"Yes, they are." said Natter, shaking his head and clenching a fist.

"If they're feeding us, then why are we fighting them?"

"They're even worse than the other tribes, don't you see? It's all part of their plan. They give us the food so we'll have strength to continue the fight, they don't let anyone die so the battles keep going on and on. They just want to watch the violence and the suffering. Well, we are going to use their system against them, wipe out and then recruit all the members of every other tribe, putting an end to these wars forever."

"Oh, right, sorry, I didn't know." I said, trying to hide my revulsion.

I have got to get away from these people.

Chapter 7 – The Raid

My little outburst didn't go down well. A man almost as big as the chief going by the name of Jumbo was assigned to accompany me wherever I went to keep me in line, which he did with all of the care and affection I would show an annoying insect. He stank of stale sweat and eyed me suspiciously, but I wasn't much better on the fragrance front after all that training. He took me to the latrine, passing a spring of brackish, pale orange water along the way.

"You don't want to drink that stuff, but it's good enough for washing."

The covering over the latrine looked to be comprised of the plastic 'canvas' of three or more tents tied onto a frame of large branches. There was a series of overlapping flat stones pushed into the soil uphill of the latrine to divert any rainwater around it and down towards the wood, but the stream bed was basically dry.

After using the latrine in the usual way, my and Jumbo's spear blades were dipped in the revolting mess and then left to dry on a rudimentary rack of Y-shaped branches under a row of lean-tos.

We then went back to the orange spring and washed our hands and faces, then followed the stream through the woods to the tent I had been assigned, all traces of my former possessions having been distributed as the Chief saw fit. It was one of a ring of eight tents around a central fireplace, and I would be sharing it with Jumbo until I could be trusted.

Jumbo filled our canteens from a nearly empty plastic box that was next to our tent and handed mine to me.

"Here. You'll be filling the box with drinking water later."

"From the waterfall by the Chief's cave?"

Jumbo slapped me hard across the face, making my ears ring. I ducked slightly and shielded my face with my arms. "What did I do? What did I say?"

"No more talk like that! That water is for the Chief, his close friends and the recruiters. We get our water from the river." Jumbo pointed to a rectangular carrying frame for the plastic box and a set of three metal pots tied to a long coil of guide rope. "But there's no approaching the river bank until recruiting is done for the day."

"OK, right, that makes sense." I looked through my hands with a wince. "Can I at least get some billow bush juice for the insect bites?"

Jumbo looked down his nose at me with a sigh and brief shake of the head, then grunted his assent and gestured in the direction of the river with his chin. We followed the now orange-brown stream towards the river, Jumbo placing a firm hand on my shoulder and pulling me down as we reached the edge of the rows of billow brushes.

"Far enough," he growled in a low voice, then crouched down beside me.

"Understood," I whispered in reply.

From my current position I could just about see that the river above the waterfall rushed through a gorge that was about ten metres wide, with sheer drops of more than five metres on either side. I couldn't see any gap in the cliffs around the bowl, and no sign of a waterfall.

"Where does the river come from?" I whispered.

"It comes out of an underground cavern at high speed right into the gorge. There's no way out that way, if that's what you're thinking."

"No, I..."

"Don't you try and play games with me. I'll be watching you until you've proven you're trustworthy, only then will we let you go out on a raid with us."

I decided that whatever I said in my defence would only make things worse, so I quietly cut myself some billow bush fronds and squeezed out the juice. After spreading it across my itching skin the irritation faded away, but my yearning to leave this place was as strong as ever.

Sometime in the afternoon, when the heat of the day was past its peak, I was 'allowed' to travel to the river's edge to retrieve some drinking water for myself and those in the neighbouring tents. By that I mean I was lowering the metal pots tied together in a vertical stack of three into a relatively still pool in the gorge ten metres below us, pulling them up and emptying their contents into the plastic box. Jumbo sat a little way from the edge and watched me out of the corner of his eye as he whittled sticks into tent pegs, chewed on a couple of grain bars, munched apples and sipped diluted billow juice from his canteen. I was allowed half a grain bar and water.

Retrieving the water was hard work and I could think of a more efficient way of doing it, but I was intent on leaving and I didn't want to help this tribe get any more capable. Besides, this way I could gain some valuable information without visibly diverging from my orders. Each time I tried to land the pots in a different part of the pool, lower them into the water until the line went slack and then count the number of arm lengths it took to bring it back to the surface, giving me a workable mental map of the water's depth.

A couple of hours later, my arms and fingers were aching and the box was half full of water.

"That'll do for now. Now we take it back."

We lifted it with the carrying frame and took it back to the space it had previously occupied next to our tent. By the time we got there my shoulders, back and legs were so sore I could do little else but lie down in my sleeping bag and rest.

"That should keep you out of trouble for a while," Jumbo said, and moved over to sit next to the fire in the middle of our circle. He sat on the other side of the fire, where he could talk to everyone else and keep his eye on me without needing to turn his head. He needn't have bothered, my eyelids were soon as heavy as my legs and arms.

There were at least a dozen people exchanging jokes around the fire, I could only see about half of them from where I was, and couldn't make out any of the punchlines, only the laughter that ensued. After a while, Jumbo broke into song, with a number of other voices joining in:

Oh a peach is soft and a cherry is sour,
A pear is as weak as a fading flower,
The plums will soon all be swept awayyyy,
Give me an apple any time of the day!

There may have been more verses to the song, but I was already asleep before they got any further.

I awoke to the sound of shouts, screams and heavy footfalls. It was pitch black outside and Jumbo was getting out of his sleeping bag. He drew two knives and scrambled out of the tent.

"What's going on?"

"We're being raided, that's probably why there was no resistance this morning, they were saving themselves for an assault. Stay here if you don't want to get stabbed."

I stayed where I was, but quietly unzipped my sleeping bag and crouched by the door flap so I could peer out at what was happening, doing what limited movement I could to loosen my aching joints. Various figures scuttled past the dim firelight. I looked around the tent for a knife, then it registered that Jumbo had them both. I saw him move forwards with a shout and took that as my cue to leave.

I picked up the glint of the little stream and charged that way, unwieldy empty box in hand. *Wait, how did I get this box? Must have been another memory wipe, some people disappearing near me.* I slowed and briefly felt around the edge of the box. It had its lid clipped on, good, but now I had no idea how close I was to the gorge.

Up ahead a box lid held like a shield caught the dim light from the stars above. I assumed there was a spear held to the left of it, so I turned my box vertically to cover as much of myself as possible, then charged at the left side of the shield, leading with the right hand edge of my box. As soon as I felt the tip of the spear glance off the bottom of the box, I shifted it back to the right to make full contact with the shield and knock my opponent onto his back, carrying on my way before he had a chance to get up or bring his spear to bear on me.

Where's the stream? There it is, keep it to the right, don't slow down. Five to fifteen metres upstream, two to six metres from the edge.

I heard a squawk of protest behind me, joined by other voices, and some heavy footsteps in pursuit. I continued running as fast as I could in the darkness, stumbling as my leg hit something rigid but flexible, falling through another set of wavy fronds as I crashed to the ground.

Billow bushes, I'm getting close.

The shouts and heavy footfalls grew closer, I picked myself up and headed away from them.

OK, find the black void in the dark, and jump into just the right part of it, or it's a ten-metre drop onto the rocks. Why did this seem like a good idea in the daylight? Where's the stream? Where's the stupid stream?

Wherever the stream was, it was masked by the billow bushes. The footfalls were getting very close now, and I continued backing away from them, until my foot missed the ground completely, and I felt myself falling over the edge.

Oh, sh –

Chapter 8 – The River

I kicked out at the cliff edge and felt some purchase, which would hopefully move me away from the rocks at the bottom of the gorge. The empty box acted as something of a sail, but before I could decide whether it was actually helping, I plunged into the water and its buoyancy wrenched it out of my hand.

The cold shock of the water made me want to gasp, but I fought the urge as I sank down to the bottom. My boots reached solid rock and I kicked myself back up to the surface, unable to see a thing. The water was relatively calm in this part of the pool, but with a stronger current ahead of me. I frantically looked around for the box, then as my eyes adjusted I caught sight of a faintly glowing rectangular form about three or four metres away – the translucent plastic of the box catching what meagre starlight reached down into the gorge differently from any other object down there.

It was rocking up and down and slowly turning. I took this to mean it would soon be picked up by the stream and swept away from me, so I swam over to it as quickly as I awkwardly could in my clothes and boots, coughing out a couple of mouthfuls of water along the way. As I reached my objective in the shallow water, the light in the gorge grew brighter, illuminating the box and the sharp rocks it was caught on more clearly. I grabbed the box and looked up. A bright white crescent, about a quarter of the size of the red one I'd seen during the day, had just appeared from behind a cloud.

Leukos?

The lip of the box seemed to have caught on the tip of a sharp rock; simply pressing down on my end of the box lifted it free.

Something hissed down out of the darkness and smashed into the rocks in front of me, the light was not only helping me see, but also making me a more visible target to whoever I knocked over. I lifted the box over to wherever the current looked strongest and dived on top of it, allowing myself to be swept downstream at a speed that I hoped would discourage my adversary from pursuing.

If he did follow me, I had enough distractions to fail to notice any further attempts to injure me. It was a wild ride over all sorts of stationary waves, hydraulic jumps, channel narrowings and widenings and sharp changes in the direction of the current. Almost every time I failed to anticipate a wave or change in direction or caught my foot on a stone, I would tip over into the water and bash my arm, leg, back or hip against an unforgiving obstacle. Each time I would keep a firm grip on the box and scramble back on top of it, putting its buoyant bulk between me and the next collision. Every so often there would be a disconcerting crunch, which I hoped was stone fragments being ground against each other rather than plastic being punctured. These incidents became more frequent as less and less light was reaching the bottom of the gorge.

Each impact on the same part of my body multiplied the pain, each climb back onto my flotation device was more tiring than the last.

The descent into deeper and deeper darkness became ever more frightening, until I began to hope that my head would take the next impact and put me out of my misery.

Just as I started to consider how to make that more likely, I caught a glimpse of a shaft of light up ahead. With the way I was being thrown about by the torrent, it was difficult to tell what it was, but as it grew closer I realised it was the end of the gorge.

Hope gave new strength to my aching muscles and I renewed my grip on the box, watching for obstacles with newfound alertness, even anticipating a wave and keeping myself upright. The channel widened and slowed as I exited the gorge into the large natural basin that fed the four waterfalls.

I was tempted to just relax and lie down on the box, then remembered that the drop into the pool was a significant height, so I slipped off into the water, trying to slow my approach and move towards the rock outcrop that split the two central falls. The current proved too strong and I went over the centre-left fall, doing my best to drop feet first and pushing the box to my right to avoid landing on it. I plunged into the deep water and its relative calm filled me with such relief that I momentarily forgot all the pain in my body.

I drifted slowly down to the bottom, just soaking in the tranquillity, looking up at the shimmering surface above me that now belonged to another, irrelevant world. Here all was beautiful, all was serene. A growing tightness in my chest reminded me that there was something this world did not have.

Air.

I kicked off the bottom and clawed my way to the surface, breathing in great gasps of cool night air, any sound I made drowned out by the roars of the nearby waterfalls. I looked around for my buoyancy aid and saw it about ten metres away, listing badly to one corner. I grunted in annoyance.

Definitely holed. Maybe if I flipped it over, or just get to the edge of this pool and move on ...

That's when I saw the flickering glow of burning torches spread along the right-hand side of the pool. I looked the other way, and there was a similar number of lights on the other side. I was surrounded. A series of expletives ran through my mind.

Are they Apples, or one of the other tribes? Even if they were, would that be any better? Killed for abandoning the Apples or killed for being one in the first place? I'll have to try and ride further down the river.

I lay as flat as I could, floating in the water, moving slowly away from the waterfalls and towards the box to avoid attracting any attention. My boots dragged me down and it required significant effort to stay afloat with them on, but taking them off was not an option since I would need them once I got back to dry land. I got to within five metres of the box, then froze in place when I heard voices at the edge of the pond:

"What's that?"

My pulse was racing.

"Looks like a food box, and with something in it."

"Go fish it out, then."

"No need, it'll be at the outflow from the pool soon, we can hook it out as it comes past. Keep a watch out for any Apples."

The light from the two torches bobbed gently as they circled around, calling to the people on the other side to come closer and narrow the gap to prevent the prize escaping them.

Inside I wanted to scream, but I trod water as quietly as I could, working against the gentle current to put distance between myself and my faithful little vessel. I heard feet splashing in the water, narrowing the gap between the torches to two or three metres as the box accelerated towards them.

There's no way I can get through there unnoticed.

A corner of the box lifted and stopped its forward motion, the opposite corner sweeping around into the middle of the outflow.

"Got it! Give me a hand back to dry land, will you? This thing is heavy."

The torches separated again.

That's better, just back off a little more, please.

"Hard luck, Sticky. Maybe next time," taunted one of the voices on the left.

"Hang on, it's leaking something." He opened the lid and looked inside. "Gah, it's just full of water from the river."

One of the voices on the right laughed. "Hard luck, Mudface. Maybe next time."

I saw the box being thrown down in disgust, ending up on the riverbank with its lid half on.

If I could just reach it ... Come on, people, there's nothing to see here, go on your merry ways.

My heart slowly sank as the torches stayed where they were. Aches and tiredness grew all over my body as I struggled to remain quiet while staying afloat. *Hang on, I'm not floating, I'm standing on an underwater rock, how did that happen?*

59

Then to my horror I began to see the first hints of light at the edge of the sky.

Got to risk it now.

I pushed off the rock towards the outflow channel, swimming as quietly as I could, lying back as still as possible and drifting with the current as soon as it gained strength. I tried to drift towards the left hand side of the outflow, to be within reach of the box on the shore, risking a sweep with my arm to turn me around and guide me that way. I instinctively froze in place as I came alongside the nearest torchlight. By what meagre flickering glimmer it gave out, it looked like it had been planted in the ground and the man nearest it was looking up the hill.

Come on, come on, there it is ...

Another sweep with my right arm as I reached out for the corner of the box with my hand, hooking my fingers to grab on to the protruding corner, but the rounded point of a shallow rock dug into my ribs and flipped me around at the last second, so my fingers bounced off the box and then I was swept past and it was out of my reach.

Dammit!

"What was that?" a voice reacted to the box rattling against its lid and my stifled grunt.

No, nothing. I winced.

"There! It's an Apple in the river, trying to get past us! Get him!"

No, no, no.

The sun peeked over the horizon and rose rapidly, revealing a short section of snaking rapids ahead of me, followed by another long still pool, with spear-wielding men spread along the banks of the river on either side.

Oh, crap.

The speed of the flow meant I was outpacing the group above me, but the downstream group started to form a human chain and spread out across the channel.

Double crap.

60

I looked around for a way out, but before anything occurred to me the current strengthened and I was pulled into the rapids.

I had managed to turn myself around during the initial calm section to be floating feet first and negotiated the first obstacle comfortably, pushing away from an upcoming rock with my boots. This got me out of alignment with the flow and soon I was tumbling completely out of control, gasping for breath every time my head came up out of the water. I scrabbled at every passing rock, but my aching fingers were unable to maintain their grip. There was a brief respite and I caught a glimpse of the still pool and complete human chain awaiting me, then my feet dropped and I was dragged down under a rock by the thunderous current.

The impact with the rock forced most of the air out of my lungs and I began to panic, thrashing around with rapidly dwindling strength, but I was pinned. The panic ebbed away, replaced by a resigned sorrow.

I am so tired, so tired. Can't I just give up now?

I opened my eyes and saw what I assumed was sunlight creeping under the rock. I reached into the gap and my fingers closed around something string-like. I pulled and found a lit beacon entangled around a small stick. Everything was going dark as I pressed the button three times. It flashed a blinding blue and then everything went black.

֍

I became aware of a bright warm light and a foul stench. I dared to open my eyes a crack and immediately closed them again, it was too much. I turned my head to the other side, in the process scraping my face against something rough but malleable. The light wasn't as bright that way, and I tried opening my eyes again.

I was on the bank of a river, I assumed it was the same river, but the water was brown and seemed to be the source of the foul smell. Out of the corner of my eye I could see a large clump of trees to my right, and that the beacon on its cord was still in my right hand, though its light was now switched off. I lifted my head from the polluted sand and found my entire body was aching, especially areas I had taken utterly for granted until now. With a series of grunts and groans that would make any octogenarian proud, I stood and surveyed my surroundings.

I appeared to be in the second-lowest half-bowl, the last one seemed to be more extended than the rest, ending in the same vertical cliffs that surrounded the whole area, but a series of vertical rock formations were spread across its width. To my left the river meandered gently up the slope, to my right it began to descend into a deepening gorge to the lip of the last bowl, either side of the gorge being heavily forested. From what I could tell, it looked like some sort of trench had been dug just in front of the distant treeline, which was crisscrossed with sturdy branches to form an imposing fence.

I looked at the beacon in my hand and pressed the button. The little light that came on, weak as it was, filled me with a certain reassurance.

Throws you back in the Gravity Ring, eh? What else were they wrong about? I'll be sure to keep you to hand at all times.

I gently shook and stretched various parts of my body this way and that, discovering what range of motion was relatively pain-free, then rolled up my right sleeve, revealing a patchwork of bruises. I tied the cord around my forearm and wrist so that the beacon would lie comfortably in my palm ready to activate at a moment's notice, then unrolled my sleeve again to mask its presence.

I began up the gentle slope of the riverbank, looking for a way around the fortified woods. As the stiffness of my limbs gradually eased, the pangs of hunger and thirst became more obvious. I looked back at the river, there was no way I was drinking from there, I'd have to look out for a stream. Surrounded by billow bushes, I tried snapping off one of the fronds to squeeze out the juice, but its high flexibility made that difficult. I looked around for a sharp stone to cut it with, but each one I came across had well-worn rounded edges. I hit upon the idea of biting the frond and tearing it the rest of the way, but as I bent down to sink my teeth into it, two men armed with spears appeared over the crest of the slope and immediately saw me. Both of them had blueberry markings on their left cheeks, but instead of a large empty circle with a small straight line, theirs was a small filled circle attached to a long curved line.

"Hey, you there, what are you doing?"

"I'm just looking for some food and water," I replied. "You wouldn't know where I could get some, would you?"

One lowered his spear at me. "Watch out! He's an Apple."

The other one did the same. "You've got a lot of nerve coming all the way out here."

"I'm not an Apple any more, I was tricked into joining them. I want nothing to do with them and escaped at the first opportunity, jumping into a gorge in the dark and nearly drowning twice."

"We've heard that before. You try to join our tribe then betray us to your friends at the first opportunity, scout out our defences or just draw us into an ambush." He called over his shoulder, "Everyone, another bit of Apple bait here! Be on the lookout for enemy forces!" A few voices beyond my line of sight acknowledged and passed on the warning.

"No, no, I don't want to join any tribe, or scout out any defences, I just want to find the lowest point in this place and get out of here."

"Let you past so you can join the Rock Eaters? No chance."

"I just said I don't want to join any tribe! What can I do to prove that I'm no threat to you?"

The one on the right moved forward with his spear. "You can let us spill your guts out on the ground."

This is not going well. I took a nervous step back. "But if you try to kill me, I'll just disappear, be healed up and thrown back in the Gravity Ring. Then when I get out the Apples will recruit me again, I won't be able to escape and I'll be made to fight you."

"You're threatening us? If we kill you quick enough, you won't make it back to the Gravity Ring."

"The only good Apple's a dead Apple, I say."

I pressed the button three times and slowly backed away. "There's no need to..."

I found myself in amongst a number of tree stumps, though there were about twice as many large trees dotted around the area. I could see that I was now in the relatively flat part of the final half-bowl, the river perhaps two hundred metres to my right and the high rock columns about five hundred ahead of me.

There was a small sharp pain in my side as I turned, I looked down and found a significant tear in my clothes and a thin red line on my skin, though it wasn't bleeding.

Looks like I was a little better at dodging blows than that white-suited guy in the Apples' woods.

In amongst the tall trees were some saplings and small trees, but none of them appeared to have any fruit on them. There were some small red fruit up in the tall trees, but all well out of reach.

Looks like all the easy stuff has been taken.

Then I noticed that the sound of splashing water that I was so used to hearing was not just in the distance to my right, but also in front of me. I rushed forward and found to my delight a small stream of clear water in a low trough.

I cupped my hands under a small waterfall and drank deeply of the cool water. It seemed to almost burn my parched throat as it rushed down, so I had to stop and take a few breaths until the drastic sensation faded, then drank deeply again, revelling in the refreshment it provided.

I sat back against the nearest tree and sighed. It felt good to just sit awhile after all of the frantic activity of the last few hours, or however long it was. The sun was quite a way above the horizon, but that didn't tell me much, since I had no idea how quickly it had been rising.

I looked back at the rock columns; there appeared to be wooden fences or fortifications of some kind around their tops with pairs of ropes strung from one summit to the next, as well as significant ground-level barricades in between the columns. There was also what appeared to be a line of dark bushes across the width of the ground in front of the columns.

Not exactly a welcoming sight. Rock Eaters? What sort of name is that?

I glanced back up the slope in the direction I had come, or rather towards the place I had been when I activated the beacon, and all thoughts of rest evaporated.

A band of five to ten men was already down the steepest part of the slope and was rapidly heading towards me, now two or three hundred metres from my position.

If the people who want me dead are afraid I'll join the Rock Eaters, then maybe I should be joining the Rock Eaters.

I stood and jumped across the trough, renewing the sharp pain in my side as I landed, then began making my way through the trees, pressing against the injury with my left hand. The stiffness in my limbs was lessening and I tried to ignore the pain as much as I could, but I was still significantly slower than my pursuers.

Once we were both clear of the trees and into the half-kilometre of open ground, it was obvious that I would be caught before reaching the safety of the rocks – if they were safe at all.

What if the Rock Eaters are even worse than the Apples? What am I getting myself into now?

This new wave of discouragement slowed my progress further, and I rubbed my temples with my free hand, causing something metallic to bash into my nose and make my eyes water. I stopped in my tracks and blinked at the offending object.

The beacon! How could I forget it was there?

I quickly fumbled it into my palm and pressed the button three times …

I found myself at the foot of a rock column. Two metres behind me was the line of bushes, averaging a metre or so high and twice as wide, covered with large thorns. My pursuers were perhaps three hundred metres away and closing. The walls of the column were pockmarked, but basically vertical, and from down here the wooden fortifications at the summit appeared insurmountable.

This is safety?

I went down on all fours and scuttled over to the edge of the nearest bush, hoping that I would be suitably hidden from my pursuers, then began crawling in the direction of the river, which was three or four hundred metres away.

I heard the footfalls and chatter of my pursuers getting closer, and I crawled a little faster.

"Fan out, he can't have gone far."

I held still and pressed the beacon again three times ... I found myself just where I was, only now I could hear my pursuers only a few metres away on the other side of the thorn bushes.

Oh, crap. Move as quietly as you can, don't give your position away ...

"Hey, you down there," called a voice from the top of the column. "What do you think you're doing?"

Double crap.

Chapter 9 – The Rock Eaters

"He's a murderer," called a voice from the other side of the hedge. "Killed two of our men then thought he could escape to you using a beacon." Two of the others were probing for gaps in the bushes with their spears.

"Is that so?" called the voice at the top of the column. "Two men, all on his own?"

"Yes, he's a tricky one. Pretended to be all friendly and harmless, then when their guard was down gutted them with their own spears, left their blood all over the rocks."

"Very impressive."

"Look at his face, he's an Apple, taught to lie and kill and steal. Let us take him away and see that he faces justice."

"It would appear that he's not too keen on that idea. You down there, what do you have to say for yourself?"

I stayed silent, not wanting to give my position away.

"Ah, you think that if you speak up, your pursuers will find you and make you disappear?"

I nodded.

"And how many of them do you think will get out of here alive if they try that? I'll wager a loaf of bread on none. Bowmen ready!"

There were various creaking and clicking noises, and five men appeared at the top of the column, plus another ten or more at the top of the neighbouring ones, each with an arrow nocked in their bows.

"Now, if you gentlemen could kindly back away, go back home and let us deal with the newcomer, then nobody needs to get hurt."

"Have it your way," said the spokesman for my pursuers as they backed away, "but I wouldn't trust him if I were you, and definitely don't turn your back on him."

"Thank you for your cooperation and your concern, but you'll excuse us if we don't take your word for it. We like to judge for ourselves."

Silence reigned for a minute or so as the two separating sides watched each other and the tension in the air ebbed away, then the man at the top of the column called down to me.

"All right, they're out of range and not coming back. What do you have to say for yourself?"

I slowly stood, peeked over the thorn bushes at the retreating forces for a few seconds, then turned to the man at the top of the column "I did face two men with spears, I was unarmed and it was on some rocks by the river. I also do carry the mark of an Apple, I'm sorry to say, I can't deny any of that. However, I was tricked into joining the Apples and escaped from them at the first opportunity, nearly drowning in the attempt. I was trying to avoid a fight with those people and I activated the beacon before any blows were exchanged, so I have no memory of what happened in the fight itself, I only know that they injured me." I showed him the tear in my clothing, I didn't think he could see the wound from up there. "I don't want to cause any trouble, just to pass through to the lowest point, wherever that is. I know this doesn't sound very convincing..."

"You'd be surprised. I know the ring of truth when I hear it."

A rudimentary panel in the fortifications swung upwards and a knotted rope was unfurled down to me, ending half a metre or so off the floor. It was different from the ropes that the Apples used, it looked a lot rougher and more ... *natural*?

"Up you come, then."

I walked up the column wall with the aid of the knotted rope, crawled through the gap and came face to face with a half-dozen men of all shapes and sizes. Some were wearing the same standard outfit as myself, others with additional or replacement crude pieces of clothing made from some sort of furry semi-rigid material. Some had the back half of their left cheek entirely filled in with blueberry markings, some had no markings at all, but each wore a proud yet warm smile on his face. They all had beards of various lengths, those with no markings having fuller facial hair than the others.

A short man with a somewhat rotund face and build extended his hand towards me, and spoke with the same voice I had heard before.

"Welcome to the Fortress."

"Thank you." I took the hand and stood, exchanged warm handshakes and welcoming greetings with the other five men, then took in my surroundings.

The fenced-in space at the top of the column was roughly five metres square, though it was more oval-shaped than anything else, with a roughly octagonal wooden shelter with a thatched roof three metres across in the middle of it. A wispy line of smoke rose from a hole in the shelter's roof, and its main supporting stakes appeared to go deep into the rock itself, with extra little wooden wedges hammered in around them to secure them rigidly in place. There was a pile of rocks in one corner of the area, next to it a plastic box half full of water, and several shields and spears leaning against the outer fence.

"How did you do that? Drive stakes into the rock, I mean?"

"We have a special tool for that, which I can show you later."

Off to each side a set of three ropes, two thinner ones hung about half a metre apart and a metre above the third, were strung from the outer fence towards other rock columns and beyond. Beyond the column to the right was a large tree, to which the ropes were secured before continuing on, but its branches hid most of what was beyond that. To the left in the distance I caught sight of a much more massive rocky plateau with a fairly irregular shape.

"These ropes, they're very different from the ropes everyone else uses, not like the tent guide ropes. Did you make them yourselves?"

He smiled and nodded. "It makes this whole fortress possible: the walls, the connecting lines, our weapons. We, or I should say our brothers across the river, make these ropes and twine from the plant that they cultivate on the far shore. In return, we grow food for them and help to construct and repair their shelters. It is perhaps not even right to consider them different from us; we all inhabit and defend the fortress that spans the valley together, bound by the same code of

70

honour, sharing knowledge, resources and cooperating on major projects."

"Grow food? You don't receive it from boxes?"

"Very rarely. Occasionally a box will arrive floating down the river, but they are usually empty, and we then use them for various purposes. One time, when our harvests were weak and the leader of the Cherry tribe was a more reasonable man, he traded a box of food they had scavenged for some bows and arrows to defend his tribe with. Here we work to support ourselves, adapting and innovating as we go; it is a much more satisfying way to live."

He gestured to the other side of the fenced area and I walked over, looking down on a great field of what appeared to be golden wheat and beside that a series of furrows and ridges covered in low-lying green leaves of various shapes. The open area of ground itself was about three hundred metres wide, right up to the cliffs at the end of the valley, and perhaps a kilometre long, from the banks of the river to the massive plateau which merged with the cliffs. Beyond the river on the other side was another similar stretch of open ground, and beyond that another plateau. The open ground next to the river on that side was dominated by a thick 'forest' of tall thin stalky plants with spiky leaves, which looked to have grown to about twice the height of the people harvesting the adjacent plot.

The river bank on both sides was fortified with a sturdy-looking high wooden fence along both banks, though on the opposite bank, it drifted a little way inland just before the river disappeared into the cliff-face, where a fair amount of branches and other floating debris looked to have gathered.

"Why is there so much debris in the river there, and what is that detour in the fence?"

"There is a sloping metal grille across the whole opening that catches large objects while letting the water through. We get a lot of building materials and most of our boxes that way, though they need to be cleaned. The detour is where the tunnel entrance is. I wouldn't go there if I were you."

"Tunnel? As in the lowest point and the way to the next stage?"

"Yes, but it's flooded all the way to the ceiling. The people we've tried sending in there either come back saying there's no way through or don't come back at all. We once tried tying a rope round an explorer's waist and sending him as far as he could go, but there was a great tug on the rope, it snapped and we never saw him again."

I gulped.

"But they wouldn't go to all this trouble just to kill us, would they? That makes no sense. I'd still like to see it for myself."

"We won't stop you from trying, but judging from all the grunting and groaning as you climbed up, I'd say you're in no fit state to make the attempt."

I glanced down at the floor. "That loud, was I?"

He sucked a little air through his teeth. "I'm afraid so. I'm sure some good food, drink, and rest will help with that. In the meantime, you can take a look around at what we've built here and see if it doesn't make you want to hang around for a while longer."

"As long as no one tries to take my beacon."

"Why would we do that? We use them all the time."

I looked up and noticed that four of the six men were wearing beacons around their necks.

"You keep them? You're not worried about being thrown … wait, that doesn't happen, does it? What do you use them for?"

"As lights, of course. They may not seem like much in the day, but you'd be surprised how much of a difference they can make at night."

I was led along the rope bridge to the next column to the left, whose upper fortification layout was much the same. My guide turned to me as we moved past its shelter.

"Do you have a name?"

"The Apples called me Hookless, but I don't like that name. I hope to find my old name once I get out of here."

"All right, then how about something more positive in the meantime, like, I don't know, Lifter? Raising moods, easing burdens, that sort of thing."

"Hmm," I nodded, feeling some of my inhibitions melt away. "That sounds a bit better, yeah, I suppose that'll do for now. What do they call you?"

"I'm Martin Grade."

I stopped where I was. "Wha – you remember your old name?"

"No, but once someone decides they're going to be here for the long term, the community comes together, they get a full name and we celebrate. Those are good days," he said with the kind of smile that made me want to see such an event for myself.

We moved on to the next column, then to the next, each of them a similar layout, though varying in size. After traversing five such columns, we arrived at the large plateau, which was around a hundred metres wide and three times as long, though with an irregular outline. The columns and their interconnecting bridges and barricades continued on into the distance, where the ground began sloping upwards towards the sides of the valley. The strip of lowland between the line of columns and the cliffs at the end of the valley was dotted with clumps of trees, partially hiding the wide stream that wound its way down the slope towards the base of the plateau.

The top of the plateau also had a fortification fence around it, and similar octagonal shelters of various sizes near its edges on top of the bare pockmarked rock, with its centre mostly empty. As we moved nearer the cliff-side, there were also rows of simple low rectangular log frames a metre or so wide, most of them filled with earth in which various edible-looking plants were growing. Shallow staircases of what first appeared to be long hollowed logs, but on closer inspection most turned out to be half-pipes of fired clay, distributed water to various locations across the surface, presumably fed by the small waterfall at the left edge of where the plateau reached the cliffs. Towards the right end of the plateau there appeared to be a cave in the cliff wall, and next to the beds of earth around us was a strange, roofless structure.

It was roughly circular and perhaps ten metres in diameter, comprised of a wide stone wall half a metre high that seemed to form the base of a three-metre fence of thick wooden stakes, all sloping inwards a little. Inhuman high-pitched noises that I couldn't quite place could be heard from the other side of the fence, and I felt mild prickles running up and down my spine. *And now we see what these people really are. What kind of twisted things are going on in there?*

"Um, what is that? A prison?"

Martin looked at me in utter bewilderment. "What? No." He then burst out laughing, shook his head, then beckoned with his left hand. "Come and see."

He walked over to a section of the fence next to where a short ladder lay on the ground, untied a short rope and swung up a panel of wooden stakes.

Inside the floor was much lower than the ground I was standing on, and gently sloped towards a crack in the rock on one side and away from what looked like a small cave on the other; the stone wall was over two metres tall on the inside all the way round. There were three women who appeared to be in their thirties in the middle of the floor, surrounded by a flock of goats. One of the women was standing and hand-feeding several of the adults with various leaves and what looked to be the tops of carrots from a wooden container. The other two were seated on battered logs, caressing and feeding kids on their laps from what appeared to be canteens with some sort of teat stretched over their normal openings. Other young and adult goats were milling around them, nuzzling the women or chasing each other and generally being adorable.

I shook my head and smiled at how wrong I'd been.

"Now this structure took the most work out of anything we've built. There was a roughly circular depression in the rock here and a crack on that side where the gap is, but we needed to hollow out the sides of the depression and build that wall so that the wooden stakes would be out of nibbling range. From experience, anything less than vertical walls will have them up and out of their enclosure, eating whatever greenery they find right down to its roots."

"If they're that much trouble, why keep them?"

"Because their regular milk and occasional meat, skins and bones are worth it. And just look at them – you wouldn't believe how much our women love those little guys." The women looked up at us, smiled and waved. I couldn't help but smile and wave back.

"I can see that, and understand it," I said with a grin. *The Apples should have tried tempting me with this instead, but there's no way they could have built it.*

"We had to lift the goats up onto the plateau, the fact they couldn't get up here by themselves is a good sign for our defences. Some of them weren't too happy about being hoisted up, and the two most troublesome males ended up as the main course of the feast we held to celebrate completing the last fortification fence. That was another good day. Since then we've been reinforcing the barrier in various ways so enemy raids are even less effective.

"This has given us the space and stability to really invest time and resources in developing tricks and mechanisms to improve everyday things, such as our shelters, water supply, the food we eat and tools we use."

In between the planting beds was a long rectangular shelter with multiple doors along one side. He gestured towards it with pride. "This is our latrine."

I looked for signs of excavation under the structure. "You dug a hole that big in the rock?"

"No, after all the trouble with the goat pen we got smarter than that. You see all the earth in the beds around us?"

"Yes, it must have taken a huge amount of work to lift up here."

"Tell me about it. So that all that effort didn't go to just a single purpose, and to slightly reduce the amount of soil needed to fill the beds, the soil is first brought here, kept as dry as possible in one of those plastic boxes. A thin layer of earth is spread in the bottom of another box, which is then slid under the seats of the latrine, two over each box. When you do your business, you take a scoop of dry soil from here and add it to what you did. This reduces the smell and at the same time fertilises the soil. When the box gets full, we slide it out, empty it into one of the earth beds then start the process again. When the earth bed gets full we plant it and construct a new one. No digging into the rock needed at all."

"Ingenious." I nodded.

"It took quite a bit of planning, implementing one of the many ideas outlined by our predecessors."

"Predecessors? How long has this community been going?"

"Our records go back five or more years, but those only began once our community was stable and secure enough to have the time and resources to begin writing them. No one knows how long it's been since the first fugitive from a roving band clambered up the secluded rock chimney, discovered the cave and waterfall and set up his hidden camp. That cave is where we store our most precious possessions."

"Your stores of food?"

"Our stores of knowledge. Which plants can be eaten, and how to recognize, cultivate and prepare them; which structures are reliable and useful for various purposes and how to build and maintain them; which tools are best for various tasks and how to make and use them; the stories and songs of our people to gladden our hearts and lift our spirits. Our first archivists wrote in the margins and blank pages of the instruction manuals they brought with them; when space ran out they moved on to scratching them into the soft stone walls of the cave. It was only when we developed the means to manufacture our own paper and had people dedicated to maintaining and adding to our records that they surged in volume and quality, vastly improving our ability to build upon previous discoveries.

"Agriculture, fabric, fire containment, irrigation, bows and arrows, light reflectors, ladders, ropes and rope bridges, traversable routes across the cliff-faces, all of these we have developed ourselves."

"Very impressive."

"Here we are, you can stay in this shelter and get some rest, I'll bring you some food."

The shelter was much the same as the ones on the column towers, small log benches dotted around most of its circumference in between rough fabric bags of straw for sleeping on.

I lay down on a bag of straw and closed my eyes. It felt so good to rest my weary limbs. Perhaps I drifted off because the next thing I knew Martin was back with a piece of flat bread and a steaming wooden bowl of some sort of stew. I couldn't tell what was in it, but it was very satisfying. A pair of peaches and a bunch of cherries followed, and I savoured the sweet flourish they provided to the meal.

"Thank you, Martin, that was very good."

"I'll pass on your compliments to the chef. Oh, there was one more thing – I'll go and get it." Martin disappeared through the shelter's doorway and came back with a small metal pot, half-filled with a familiar purple liquid …

I backed away. "What are you going to do with that?"

"Offer it to you."

"What for?"

"So you can blot out your Apple markings, if you want."

"Won't that make me one of you?"

"It doesn't have to. It'll just mean that you renounce your former allegiance, that you're nobody's property, and nobody has to know who you were allied with before. Just spread it on your cheek, obscuring whatever is there now. Over time it'll all fade to nothing."

I looked at the bowl, slowly reached out and dipped the fingers of my left hand in the sticky liquid, then smeared it all over the back of my left cheek, in my mind telling all the Apples to go and jump in the river. I looked up at Martin with half a smile.

"That felt good."

He smiled back. "I'll bet it did."

My smile faded a little. "I, I have a question, though."

"And what's that?"

"Now, I know you've all achieved a lot here, but isn't there more beyond the tunnel? Isn't there a much larger body of knowledge to build on out there, beyond this stage? Think of what we know they can do: they make all those boxes, tents, beacons, clothes and food; they construct truly astounding projects – the Gravity Ring, The White Space and this valley; they can even heal great injuries and wipe our memories. Who knows what else they can do, what we could be part of, if we just take that risk?"

"But here we have control of our destinies, here we are feared by the barbarians, we're making great progress and provide much-needed stability to the valley. If we abandon all of this and risk the tunnel, what will happen to the fortress, to this haven, to this family? It will be occupied by a bloodthirsty tribe and used to terrorise everyone else here."

"I suppose so, but is this really meant to be our home, our final destination? They lured us out of the Gravity Ring with the promise of great adventures to be had and a real world to discover, and told us where to find the way out of here. There is clearly more to the real world than this valley, and out there is a world full of greater wonders than we can imagine.

"You have been here five, maybe ten years. How long have they been out there, a hundred, a thousand, ten thousand? If you can make all of this progress in the short time you have been here, just imagine how much progress they have made in theirs. You've made a lot of discoveries, I'll grant that, but do you really need to rediscover what they already know out there, and I assume are willing to share? Think of all the songs and stories they've written, the secrets they've discovered, places they've been, structures they've built and devices they've developed. That is something to explore and build on, out there, in the real world."

"Are you sure they would share? What if they are like the other tribes here? Everything we've toiled and sweated for, all we've achieved and worked to build and defend, it would be for nothing, sacrificed for a foolish hope. We would be nothing to them – a plaything, easy prey. I'll take my chances here with the freedom we've built."

"But if this is where our journey is not supposed to end, then yes, you'll lose all you've built here, but with all the tenacity, industry and creativity you clearly possess, you'll be able to replace it all and more out there, won't you?"

"That's easy for you to say, you've invested nothing here. You haven't seen your plans come to fruition and felt the surge of pride when the last part is secured into place, your creation is put to use and the first beneficiary smiles in gratitude. Build with us, taste that joy and then tell me you want to leave it all behind."

I stared into space for a while as I considered the idea. *Risk the tunnel, or help these people? Flee the valley, or stay and build?* I looked up at him.

"All right. You seem to be good people, I hope you'll think the same of me. I had an idea that might help me live up to that name you gave me …"

Chapter 10 – The Project

Martin leant forward. "Alright, then, Lifter, I'm all ears."

" Well, I'd need to see how you lift things up onto the plateau, but I think I have an idea for a mechanism to make it easier. I'd have to look around the perimeter for a suitable place to build it, and it'd need one or two plastic boxes, ideally more. Also," – I patted my pockets and felt a small bump in one of them, put my hand inside and retrieved a small translucent disc with rounded edges – "I was looking for a good place to plant this when I was tricked into joining the Apples. Here looks to be as good a place as any."

"What's that, a disparity tree seed?"

"'Disparity tree'? Is that its name?"

"Well, that's the name our predecessors gave it. Quite a remarkable plant: a beautiful display it puts out, delicious fruit and its sap makes for a useful adhesive. We have a little cluster of them growing down below the plateau on the other side, so we have plenty of seeds; no need to give us that one. Keep it as a souvenir, if you like."

"Oh. Though, wouldn't it be better to plant it up here, so you don't have to carry the fruit up?"

"Trees don't do well up here, the soil isn't deep enough for them in the beds. Anyway, I'll show you our little lifting rack, then if you think you can do better, I can take you to the archivists."

I was taken to a gap between two outcrops, where a sturdy log spanned a cleft in the rock, the log seemingly half-buried into the surface of the plateau on both sides of the precipice. There were two ropes two or three metres apart slung over the log that hung down on one side and their other ends went out horizontally out across a long open stretch of the plateau. The sections of the log where the ropes hung over it were coated with plastic, which I was told was carefully melted from a pair of broken box lids, and the laid out sections of rope had pairs of loops attached to them at roughly two-metre intervals, with a two- to three-metre branch tied between the ropes just before the loops began.

"We have twelve guys put the loops over their shoulders and together they drag the rack up the cleft in the rock. The usual loads are boxes of soil, produce from our fields or orchards, or cut logs for construction materials. If you take a look over the edge, you can see what the rack itself looks like."

I leant on the fence and looked down. Thin logs had been lashed together into an approximation of a raft with a rail around it, and the ropes joined two others that led to each of its corners. Up at the top of the cliff, there was a ledge in the rock about two metres below the log, with a shallow slope from there up to the upper surface of the plateau.

"How difficult was the rack to make? Could you make a second one? And add a second log up here?"

"Why would we want to do that?"

"Well, I was thinking of attaching the two of them to the ends of a single set of ropes across the logs, putting two plastic boxes on the new platform. We could then sometimes divert the flow from the waterfall to fill the boxes, and their weight would pull down on one side, pulling up what's on the other. Get the balance right, and you'll have almost no lifting work to do at all."

"Nice, but what if we don't get the balance right? Wouldn't one side come crashing down and break the whole thing?"

"We'd need to have a rope attached to each side with a couple of people taking the strain on each, so that whichever side is heavier can be pulled up or slowly let down. Also, we'd have to make sure that the bottom side is filled first, and then the water side, with some ability to stop or divert the water away quickly so it doesn't go too far past the balance point. With practice, we'll be able to establish some standard balance points to use."

"Sounds like you've put a bit of thought into this."

"It came to me when I was lifting water up from a gorge potful by potful for the Apples."

He grinned. "Nothing motivates you to improve efficiency like a bit of monotonous toil. It all sounds very good, I'm sure we can get a lot of rings together for it."

"Rings?"

Martin slapped himself on the head. "Oh, right, I forgot all about it." He reached into a pocket and took out a few white plastic rings. "These are favour tokens; we make them by carefully melting down broken box lids. They can be split into four by cutting them with a knife, but any smaller than that and they become worthless. Everyone starts with ten when they arrive, and whenever you do a favour for someone, they will give you a quarter ring or two, or even a whole one if they really value what you've done for them. We can't afford to have any parasites here, and this is the best way to see who is actually contributing.

"Everyone also gives a quarter ring each day to that week's watch chief, so that the people manning the fortress walls can get a whole ring for each day they spend on watch. Henry at the archives can sketch out your idea and give you your starting rings – he's over this way."

ⱷ

Martin went around the camp, enthusiastically telling people about my plan and showing them Henry's simple schematic, in all getting together over forty rings towards its construction. Trees were chopped down with flint axes, logs cut to length with simple saws made of bone, fibres woven together into strong ropes and used to tie the logs together as well as looped over the support logs.

The second great support log was lifted up onto the plateau using their existing system, then the central sections where the ropes would be hung were coated with plastic in the same way. It was slowly rolled into place, where indentations to fit its girth had been hacked out of the rock with a large iron pickaxe, and fine shaping was done by hammering metal pegs into the edges of the hole and then scooping out the rubble.

"Where did you get that pickaxe from? Did you make it yourselves?" I asked as I tied together a support frame for one of the new water channels together with Martin Grade and Jason Frank, a tall and square-jawed man with a love for all things structural.

Jason looked at the implement and sighed. "Our predecessors made that. It was buried in sand and rubble from when part of the roof of the cave collapsed, together with a hammer and their records of all of their discoveries, including how to extract metal from the right type of stone using a strong charcoal fire in a column of clay bricks. We've been able to surpass them in every way except one; we haven't been able to make a metal as hard and resilient as that. There must be some trick they didn't write down; we'll figure it out eventually. The metal we can make is good for other things, like cooking implements, pegs, and light reflectors."

As he turned to point towards the cave, the flat piece of polished bone he wore on a string around his neck – which looked something like a cracked piece of eggshell – shifted its position and caught my attention. I'd seen a few people wearing them, I assumed they were some sort of tribal marking and I was just about to ask him about it when a beautiful and shapely woman with long brown hair approached us. She wore a warm smile, carrying a pot of steaming stew, four wooden bowls and two loaves of bread on a wooden tray. She had a beacon around her neck, to which was tied a similar-shaped piece of polished bone to the one Jason wore.

"Are you hungry, my love?"

"That looks delicious, but not as appetising as you, Jay." Jason opened his arms and her smile widened.

She set down the tray on a nearby pair of logs, sat down on his lap, put her arm around his shoulders and kissed him on the forehead, then looked at our work.

"How's it going?"

"Very well, we've been showing Lifter here how to tie the struts together for maximum stability, he's a quick learner. If we can convince him to stay, he'll be my assistant in no time," he said with a grin, then registered that I was staring at the woman on his lap with my mouth open slightly. "Oh, Lifter, this is Jane." Jason held up his piece of polished bone, and Jane did the same. The two pieces slotted together to form an oval with a tree symbol etched across it.

"Mrs Jane Frank." She smiled and kissed him on the top of his head.

"You two are … married?"

"Five weeks tomorrow," she said with pride.

"I'm the luckiest man in the fortress." Jason beamed and kissed her on the cheek.

"I, I, certainly can't argue with that." I said, blushing as I felt a pang of loneliness, then turned to Martin. "How many married couples are there here?"

Martin glanced down at his hands and briefly counted on his fingers, but as he did so I caught a glimpse of that same pain in his eyes.

"Oh, at least thirty. Henry would know, he keeps the records. The ceremonies often coincide with people declaring they'll stay with us, so they choose their full names at the same time. Having marriages has really helped to stabilise our community, but we've found that once a couple gets married, something changes." He stared into space. "Their fates are tied together; when one of them disappears, the other does as well, and we never see them again."

Jane and Jason's smiles faded a little and they exchanged nervous glances, then Jane brightened as she sought to change the subject:

"Talking of Henry, did I just see him hollowing out a log back there?"

"Oh, yes," said Jason with a fresh smile. "He was so excited about the project, he couldn't wait to get outside and be a part of it."

Jane turned to me with a nod and a smile. "Be proud, Lifter, you've achieved something very rare."

The work progressed steadily over the next couple of days, the slowest part of the process being the production of enough fired clay half-pipes for the new water channel, especially since a couple were tragically dropped on the way to their support frame, breaking into too many pieces to be salvageable.

Finally, in the early afternoon of the third day, all was set up and a significant crowd had gathered to witness the first test run. All the lengths of rope that would come into contact with the logs had been coated in oil extracted from one of the crops grown on the other side of the river. Four men were hooked into the loops on each horizontal rope, the team on the right rope about ten metres further back than the one on the left, and a test cargo of a closed half-full box of soil had been placed on the lower rack, which was resting on the ground. Two empty boxes were on the upper rack, and a short hollowed log that split into two channels was just above them, one channel leading into each box.

Martin raised a hand and called out, "Both sides gently take the strain!"

The two teams of men walked slowly backwards a few steps, until both ropes were off the ground.

"Once again, shout out 'shift!' as soon as you feel a change in the tension in your rope. Open the upper gate!"

The command was quickly echoed along a human chain to a junction in the water channel, where a thin block of wood attached to a loop of rope was pulled out of one slot in a hollowed log and a second such block lowered into the other, shutting off the normal flow into the irrigation system and diverting it into the new channel. There were no leaks along the channel this time, all previous holes having been sealed with wet clay.

The silvery flow spread quickly down the slope, the ripples that flowed out from each little downward step reflecting back and forth off the walls of the channel as the water level steadily rose, meeting another closed gate that diverted the flow to the right, down a channel that led away from the shallow slope and poured down the corner of the cleft in the rock, well away from the plastic boxes.

"Overflow channel is working properly," the man standing next to it reported.

"Close the overflow and open the lower gate."

The block above the overflow channel was lowered into its slot and the gate that had previously diverted the flow that way was opened, the water rushed through the diverging half-pipes and into the boxes, though some still leaked down the overflow channel. The man nearest the upper rack steadied it with a long hooked staff as the boxes filled, the ropes connecting the two racks creaking as the strain on them grew, yet there was no sign of movement. Both boxes reached about a quarter full, then maybe a third full.

"Must be getting close now. Open the overflow channel, and close the lower gate halfway."

The flow into the boxes slowed a little as the cascade from the overflow resumed, and after a little while the ropes shifted a little, the rope to the further team of men jumping up, and the rope of the nearer team dropping slightly.

"Shift!" came the cry from both teams as their men adjusted their feet.

"Close the lower gate! Close the upper gate!"

The order was relayed up the slope as before, and the upper gate was closed. However the block of the lower gate caught on something on the way down and jammed into its slot at an angle, refusing to budge up or down, and the water continued to flow into the boxes. The members of the far team leant further back as the strain on their rope increased.

"Get some more men on that rope and block the lower gate!"

Another three men grabbed onto the end of the rope behind the far team while men near the lower gate stuffed branches and leafy twigs into the gap. They scooped stones and potfuls of soil onto the branches until the flow through the gate reduced to almost nothing, and all the remaining water flowed down the overflow channel. One of them reached over to the upper rack and scooped water out of the boxes with a metal pot until the further team was happy with the load. The far team walked slowly forwards and the nearer team backwards, both with smiles on their faces at how little effort it took to lift the box of soil up to the top. Once there, the lifting rack was hooked with the staff and drawn over to the ledge, where the box was slid off, placed in a carrying frame and carried up the shallow slope.

There were a series of cheers from the onlookers and Martin came over to me and slapped me on the back. "Apart from the lower gate, that worked very well. We've had problems with water gates before; we'll just sweep the rubbish out, find the protrusion and chisel it out."

The problem was found and fixed in half an hour, another seven loads were lifted using the new system, and the workday was declared over. I was later told that we had managed twice the normal daily workload overall, which was a good sign considering how little of the day had been left. We discussed plans for putting markings on the boxes to more accurately tell how full they were, an alternative lower gate design to better control the flow rate, and for a balance beam at the bottom of the lift for estimating the amount of water needed to counterbalance a given load. Those would be projects for another day.

That evening I sat around a large fire next to the residential shelters as stories were exchanged, drinks shared and songs sung. One stood out, sung by a pair of lilting female voices that drifted across the plateau:

From troubles deep my heart did flee,
In search of life so full and free.
By fertile fields, in a fortress strong,
I found the place where I belong.

Here in the Haven, my family
My favourite part of humanity;
We work together, we grow and build
With strong wills, strong backs, and fingers skilled.

My soul was lonely, all full of fear
At shadows far and dangers near;
With trembling knees was forced to roam,
'Til alongside you I found my home.

Here in the Haven, my family
My favourite part of humanity;
We work together, we grow and build
With strong wills, strong backs, and fingers skilled.

So now you watchmen upon her wall
Be on your guard so she won't fall.
So many strive to break her gate
To loot, destroy and violate.

Here in the Haven, my family
My favourite part of humanity;
We work together, we grow and build
With strong wills, strong backs, and fingers skilled.

I looked around at all of the happy faces seated around the fire, and thought to myself with a smile, *Yeah, I can see why people would want to call this their home.*

I cast my mind back to the brief glimpses I'd had of the tunnel entrance and my smile faded.

But not me.

Chapter 11 – The Tunnel

The next morning, Martin led me to the edge of the plateau, where a rope spread out across the cliff-face, tied to metal pegs hammered into the rock. Below the ledge was a line of half-pipes that carried water to a rocky spot near the river, where it fell down in a waterfall that was used to clean debris collected from the metal grille. We traversed the cliff-face over the river mouth, reaching a half-metre square ledge on the other side, next to which a knotted rope hung from a rock protrusion, secured in place with a couple of pegs. I climbed down after Martin, and found myself at the entrance to the tunnel. The footprints of dried mud up its sloping floor that disappeared into the darkness seemed to beckon me in.

"Well, here you are. This is what you wanted, wasn't it? Still want to risk it?"

"I don't think I could live with myself if I didn't. Thank you for all of your help."

I opened my mouth to say something else, then closed it again. *No, I need to say it.*

"Martin, I saw the way you looked at Jason and Jane the other day, the way you envied them. Who wouldn't? There's nothing stopping you, is there, from coming with me? I mean, how do you know there isn't someone waiting for you on the other side?"

Martin sighed and spoke quietly. "Look, I know you mean well, but we've had this discussion. I won't stop you, you're welcome to try and get through the tunnel, but I … I belong here. Here I'm important, I make a difference. These people are my friends. They put themselves in harm's way to help me, and I happily do the same for them. I can't just leave them, not like that. It's better for them that I stay."

I nodded. "I understand, and respect your reasons for staying." I held out a hand. "I wish you all the best with your life here, but I just can't imagine living so close to the tunnel, not knowing what's on the other side."

Martin shook my hand with a strong grip. "I understand and respect your reasons for going. Good luck, I hope you find the name you're looking for."

"Thank you."

I took the remaining plastic rings out of my pocket and placed them on a rock by the tunnel entrance. I took a deep breath, then switched my beacon's light on and stepped inside. The ceiling was a good two and a half metres high, there was no need to stoop, and I made my way up the slope. The stench of the river faded away the deeper I went, being replaced with the slightly salty and metallic fragrance of the cave's walls. The remaining traces of dried mud crunched quietly under my feet as I approached a crest in the path. The light from the beacon was just enough to see all around me and appeared to be getting stronger, or maybe it was my eyes adjusting to the gloom, and small crystals in the rock walls caught the light in various ways as I passed them.

I reached the crest and looked back. The circle of daylight was about ten or twenty metres away now, all I could see of Martin was his feet, but it looked like he hadn't moved since we shook hands, not even to pick up the rings. *Is he expecting me to turn back?*

I peered ahead, where the tunnel started descending again, and the floor began to be a lot more reflective. Ahead a little further and I saw the source – an utterly still and clear pool of water that the tunnel descended down into all the way to the ceiling. It thankfully appeared to be a lot cleaner than the water in the river, the rocks at the bottom of the pool being perfectly visible. I stepped into the water and felt the moisture soak through my clothing. It was cold, but not unbearably so. I descended lower and lower, stopping as the beacon dipped below the surface and the underwater world became more brightly illuminated.

I took a few deep breaths, then closed my eyes and ducked under the water. As soon as I did, I had the sensation of being pulled down and thrown about by a swirl of chaotic currents. I thrashed with my arms and pushed with my legs, finding purchase on the floor and bursting up through the surface to find myself exactly where I'd been, panting heavily, the only ripples in the water being those caused by my own thrashings.

What was that? What just happened?

I took another few deep breaths and went down again. I felt the same need to thrash out, immediately stood up again and all was calm. I looked back up the tunnel the way I'd come. *Do I turn back? Tell them they were right, and there's no way through?*

I imagined Martin welcoming me back, taking me up to the plateau where I'd live out the rest of my days defending and improving the fortress. The Haven. A good life, the best in the valley. I looked back at the tunnel ceiling disappearing into the water, its cold mystery mocking my fearfulness.

One more try.

I waited for the waves to die down and this time I went down slowly with my eyes open. I flinched again as the water closed around my head, but I could see that the water itself was calm and I fought the urge to thrash about again. About five or six metres ahead of me there was a large boulder on the floor of the tunnel, but more than enough of a gap on the right side of it to get past. Beyond that, the tunnel continued under the water, but it was difficult to see where it went.

I stood up and took a few deep breaths then went back under, suppressed the urge to panic and moved over to the boulder. The tunnel's ceiling rose up above the boulder, meeting a gently undulating reflective surface about half a metre wide and two long, above which nothing was visible. I stood on the boulder and slowly poked my head up through the surface.

I found a small pocket of stale but still breathable air, the rock only rising a metre or so above the water before curving back down again. I took a few breaths before ducking back down, again suppressing the urge to fight as the water closed over my head and looked at the tunnel ahead. It carried on at the same level for another ten or so metres, then turned to the left out of sight.

All right, go to the corner and take a look, then kick off that far wall and come back here.

I stood up for one more breath, then slipped down and pushed off the boulder, doing an approximation of breaststroke with my arms. On reaching the corner, I looked to my left and saw that about five or so metres past the far wall of the original tunnel, the floor sloped up and emerged from the water completely. I disregarded my original plan and kicked off the right wall towards this new exit, breaching the surface and taking a few deep breaths of fresher, but still salty air.

Made it, yes! I clenched a fist in celebration, then began to laugh, which echoed throughout the cave. "No way through, is there?"

The tunnel rose up for another ten metres or so to another crest, though I could hear what sounded like running water on the other side. I ascended the slope and beyond the crest found the ceiling lowering much more sharply than the floor, reducing the floor-ceiling distance to a metre or less, forcing me onto my hands and knees to go further.

The ceiling got no higher, and the sound of rushing water grew louder.

You've got to be kidding me!

The tunnel ended two metres ahead of me, the only exit being an approximately one-metre diameter channel all the way across the floor, filled with a smooth but rapidly moving body of water, both ends of the channel being pitch black and below the level of the floor.

I placed my hand in the water, which was warmer than the previous pool, and the current was very strong. There would be no way back if I climbed in there, I might not even be able to stop myself from falling in if I put my head under to take a look.

I thought of the men in white, of whoever decided to arrange things this way. "You people are sick! Why would you do this to me?" I sighed. *This must be why people either give up or never come back.*

I looked back the way I had come.

So, which is it to be?

I rested my forehead on the rocky floor, my knuckles whitening as I considered the possibility of dropping into the water and being swept away, utterly out of control, my breathing coming in heavy sobs.

No, no, no, no, yes, *do it!*.

My ambition grabbed onto the small window of sanity, if that's what it was, and I rolled over into the stream before I could change my mind again.

"No!" I coughed and thrashed as I hit the water, the strong pull of the current being all too reminiscent of my previous ordeal, but in doing so I let out a precious half-lungful of air before sinking.

The tunnel I was swept into turned downwards and narrowed as the flow accelerated, the water filling the whole of its diameter in a chaotic opaque mass; there was nowhere to grab another breath. Down and down, faster and faster, twisting and turning. I scrambled at what I hoped was the wall, but there was nothing to grab onto. I bumped into a wall, but was numb to the pain of it, merely losing another precious bubble of air with the impact. On and on it flowed, with no end in sight.

This is taking too long ... too long ... too ... long ...

Everything faded to black ...

"Name?" asked a male voice in the darkness.

94

It was then that I realised that there was no sound or sensation of rushing water. I reached for my beacon to turn on its light, but it wasn't there. I wasn't in the water any more, in fact I was completely dry and warm, lying in some sort of bed. Waiting for my eyes to adjust didn't help, there seemed to be no light to adjust to.

"Name?" the voice repeated.

"What?"

"What is your name?"

"I don't know."

"Then choose one. You cannot be admitted further without a name."

"Wait, wait, I was told I could stay nameless for the rest of my days. Were you lying to me?"

"We were not. It is perfectly acceptable to remain without a name for as long as you live in the Wilderness Stage, which some choose to do for the rest of their days. You have chosen to return to civilised life, and you cannot function in society without a name."

"Then what about my old name? I came here to rediscover who I am and where I come from, as well as what brought me here. You must know who I was."

"The person you were is gone, dead. That life destroyed itself in a way that is now irrelevant. You have a fresh start; who you are and will be will depend on your choices and actions from this point forward."

"But how can I learn from my mistakes if I don't know what they were? I have to know who I was, what I did that was so terrible. Tell me, please. I can handle it, whatever it was."

"I do not have that information, no one here does. No records are kept of who you were; the only records about you will begin when you choose your new name."

My heart sank. *No records, no history, no roots. Everything gone. Nothing left.* "Choose my own name, just like that? How can I? How can I define myself?"

"Think about what you have learned about yourself during your time in the Wilderness Stage, and what sort of man you want to be, then choose your name accordingly. In your own time peruse these lists of names, their meanings and histories, and make your choice."

Pale-brown faintly glowing text appeared to my left on the otherwise black wall two to three metres away from me, providing enough light for me to see that I was dressed in white overalls.

```
Name Search Options:

First Name/Family Name

Search Alphabetically

Search by Meaning

Search by History

Search by Profession
```

A dull light began to emanate from every part of all four flat walls and the ceiling, revealing a black reclining chair in front of the black screen, with a low dark brown table next to it on which lay a notepad and pencil, a blue plastic cup of water and a plate of neatly sliced sandwiches. The light grew gradually brighter, so my eyes had plenty of time to adjust without it ever being uncomfortable. There was no one else in the room and no visible exits, the voice came from the ceiling.

"Simply speak your commands to the screen, and it will provide you with the information you require. Take as long as you need."

I sighed, defeated. *What can I do? What chance do I have against them and all of their wonders?* I turned and stood up from the bed, pleasantly surprised to find no aches and pains in any part of my body as I moved. I placed both hands on the back of the chair as I considered the options.

Who am I, and who do I want to be?

Chapter 12 – Into the Light

After several hours, I worked my way down to a list of three potential first names and two family names.

Unable to decide between them, I span the pencil between the two family names, resolving to select whichever one it ended up pointing at. When it ended up pointing at the name on the left, I found myself feeling disappointed.

"Hmm," I grumped. "Hang on, I don't need to obey this thing, do I? I'll just choose the other one, Walker it is. I walked out of the Gravity Ring, and I'll persevere, come what may, on my own two feet." I then imagined the pencil spinning between the first names, and thought about which I would prefer it to end up on. I laughed at myself and shook my head. "That was easy, wasn't it? Zephyr, of the west wind, so I'll always remember where I came from."

"My name is Zephyr Walker."

"Thank you, you are now registered. Please make your way to the exit."

"What ex—" I stopped as a section of the wall to my left folded away with a faint breath to reveal a rocky tunnel, the only light in it appearing to come from the room I was in. I stepped into the doorway and looked up and down the tunnel, seeing a distant source of daylight to my right.

The slightly reflective rocky floor showed me that there were no obstacles between me and the exit. I made my way towards it, shielding my eyes as I reached the opening. Various scents and sounds gradually replaced the echoing dry saltiness of the tunnel.

The glare became bearable. I was in a magnificent garden with oval and rectangular flower beds, perfectly trimmed lawns and hedges; ornate fountains and statues, stone-lined sandy paths, ponds and waterfalls; and orchards of all sorts of trees. It was walled on three sides by a horseshoe of high rocky cliffs up which vines, flowers and occasional grassy clumps grew, and in the distance on the fourth side by a great sandstone building incorporating multiple ornate columns, arches, spires and stained-glass windows. In large letters above its main central arch was inscribed the question:

WHAT IS THE GOOD AT WHICH ALL THINGS AIM?

The nearest metallic statue was of a robed man addressing an audience, one hand held an open book and the other pointed to the sky. The sound of the sandy path crunching under someone's feet caught my ear, and I looked up to see a man approaching in a pale brown suit with a green floral sash.

"Greetings, Zephyr, I am Professor Brown."

"You know my name?"

"It was sent to me the moment you registered." He showed me a silvery wristband, above which hovered an image of my face together with the words Zephyr Walker.

"Wow, how does that work?"

"It is called a holoband. I'm no expert on technological matters, there are others here who could explain its mechanism far better than me, I only know how to use it." He pointed a finger at my image then at himself, causing my name to light up in green, then with a flick of the same finger scrolled through several other faces and names, nodded his head then tapped a panel on the wristband to switch the display off.

"There. You are now assigned to my care."

"So, Professor Brown, was it? What is this place?"

"This is the gateway to civilised life, otherwise known as the Academy."

"Gateway, so I can just walk through there out into the real world?"

"In theory, but we would be doing you a great disservice to send you out there unprepared. At the Academy, you will receive instruction in the basics of civilised life, together with training towards a profession of your choice based on an assessment of your talents. After that we will help you find work in that field and temporary accommodation, from where you will be free to move wherever you wish as soon as you can afford to do so."

"That sounds good, I must admit, but I have to ask, did you have to wipe away who I was? Why all these different stages?"

"That will be covered in the first of your lectures, but to satisfy your understandable curiosity, a little history is in order. A long time ago, long after this colony had become comfortably established and its citizens were able to enjoy a life of ease, there arose a group known as the nihilists: followers of a disastrous philosophy that occasionally plagues mankind.

"They believed that there is no such thing as objective reality, no beauty, truth, honour, morality, or value of any kind. Accordingly, they created nothing of their own, but only sought to deface, distort or destroy the work of others. They protested against all forms of responsibility, rejoiced in senseless violence and depravity; would curse the praiseworthy and praise the despicable, aiming to eliminate all sense of worth, all reasons for gratitude, all traces of hope. After a particularly heinous crime that disfigured two hundred children, our authorities seized all the leaders of the movement and intended to execute them.

"One of our philosophers suggested a different solution, that they be placed in cryogenic suspension until we could provide them with a world that their philosophy demanded. An environment where there would be no physical reality to interact with: no sights, sounds, textures or smells. We would wipe their memories of the outside world so that their philosophy could have every chance to be justified. There would be only vague hints of there being something beyond the mist, in the hope that they would reject such a reality and begin the path back to life."

"The Gravity Ring."

"Correct."

I began to feel nauseous. "So I was one of them? I was a Nihilist? I did those terrible things?"

Professor Brown held up a reassuring hand.

"No, not necessarily, let me finish. To reject the Gravity Ring is to reject the utterly easy and safe life, in all its tedium. Once out of the Gravity Ring, the Wilderness Stage is intended to gradually reintroduce various realities, such as the beauty of nature, value of cooperation, progress and basic civilization, as well as something of how our ancestors lived so that modern conveniences will be appreciated rather than taken for granted. The philosophical descent into nihilism was a gradual process, so it was thought best to reintroduce such realities in stages. In this way, those content with rudimentary civilization – such as tribal life in all its violence, or the insular community of the fortress – are quarantining themselves from the rest of society. They only move on and come to us once they outgrow those pale imitations and are ready and keen to relearn what wisdom we have to pass on.

"The programme proved so successful in reforming the Nihilist leaders that it was not only also used on lower ranking members of the movement, but also expanded to take in those who sought to destroy themselves or society in other ways: murderers, the suicidal, those who made their living through wanton violence, theft or deception. One such downward spiral brought you here. It does not matter which one, you now have a fresh start and a clean slate."

My face fell and I stared at the floor. *What sort of monster was I?*

The professor placed a hand on my shoulder and looked me in the eye. "I know that look. That downward spiral ended when you entered the Gravity Ring. Whoever you were has paid his debt, he is gone. Who you are now can do great things and has a whole world of opportunities ahead of him. Come, let me show you to your room."

The walls of my room, like those of the corridors, were covered with carved wood panels inscribed with intricate floral patterns. It had a large bay window overlooking the gardens, housed a single bed with small en-suite bathroom, a chair and desk with a screen and keyboard, largely empty bookshelf and a wardrobe and chest of drawers next to a two-person sofa.

"If you're not keen on being dressed all in white, there are a few things to choose from in there – they should all fit you."

I looked through the wardrobe and picked out an electric blue top and pale blue trousers, at least that was what their labels said.

"Very good, but feel free to change what you wear from day to day."

"What happened to my beacon?"

"It was recharged and sent back to the White Space, where it will serve to light the way for someone else. You will not need it here – there is little in the way of danger, and help is much closer to hand when required."

"So how did the request for help work with the beacon, and how is it done here? I know that it involved some sort of memory wipe …"

"Correct, the emergency function included an induced temporary anterograde amnesia."

"A what?"

"Again, I am no expert in these things, but when the beacon's rescue function is activated, it gives a burst of radiation that affects everyone within line of sight, temporarily disrupting the part of the brain that consolidates short-term memory into long-term memory. This means for a period of approximately two minutes, whatever is no longer the focus of your immediate attention is quickly forgotten. During that two-minute window, a rescue team equipped with gravity packs is dispatched to retrieve the individual requesting help, whether that is to take them to our medical facility or simply relocate them to another part of the valley.

"Here in the Academy you can request help via holoband. Later today, you will be provided with one with basic functionality: communication, reference, navigation and departmental access, and there will be a limited range of styles to choose from. There is no strict dress code at the Academy, but we do insist on punctuality. Your introductory lecture begins in an hour, just follow the signs for Lecture Hall Ten.

"Then will come lunch, you'll receive your holoband and be given an initial tour of the Academy. Tomorrow we will begin your instruction in basic philosophy, ethics and social etiquette. After that we will give you overviews of history, economics, the natural sciences and engineering, before giving you your general assessment and advising you on potential career paths. Once you have chosen a path, we will provide you with appropriate training and contacts with employers in that field, as well as access to various recreational, sports and self-defence programmes. Do you have any questions?"

"It's a lot to take in at once, but there was one thing: when I was with the Apples, I saw one of your operatives attacked, and found his blood all over one of the trees. Is he all right?"

"He has made a full recovery, and learned not to overstay his two-minute welcome in the valley – especially not without a helmet."

"I am glad to hear that, but it sounds like a very painful lesson to learn."

"Many important ones are. An intelligent man learns from his mistakes, a wise man from the mistakes of others."

"Then I'll try my best to be the latter. Where is it I need to be in an hour, room ten?"

"Lecture Hall Ten, yes. Just make it there in time and everything else will be taken care of. Good luck in your studies, I'll see you in class."

"Thank you."

He departed with a smile and closed the door.

I took in the pattern of subtle floral silhouettes on the walls, then tested the sofa. It was just as luxurious as I remember the sofa in the White Space being, and the bed was even softer, seeming to mould itself to my prone form and invite me to drift off to sleep. I reluctantly stood and examined the en-suite bathroom. It was tiled with polished stone and equipped with a flush toilet, crystalline basin and large enclosed shower cubicle.

I lifted the silvery handle over the basin and a warm liquid spiral rushed out of the pipe. *Water to hand whenever you want it, and warm as well, nice.* The base of the handle was blue on its right side and red on the other. I pushed the handle as far as it would go to the blue side and the flow quickly became icy cold. Pushing it all the way to the other side and it became almost scalding hot. Back to the middle and it was the same comfortable warmth I'd started with. I looked around at the other bathroom appliances and grinned to myself. *I'll have to try the rest of this out soon.* I dried my hands with the luxurious towel provided and then headed out to my first lecture.

Three days later, ten of us were sitting in a circle while the visibly pregnant young woman to my left read from our assigned text.

" ' ...These states of character, then, are vices; yet they do not bring

disgrace because they are neither harmful to one's neighbour nor very

unseemly.' "

"Thank you, Stephanie. Were there any questions before we move on to Pride?"

I raised my hand, and the professor gestured towards me. "Please."

"Well, it is clear to all of us that this program, these facilities, the Gravity Ring and Wilderness Stage, they must have cost a vast amount of resources to construct, and a lot to run. Would that be magnificence, or vulgarity?"

The professor smiled. "Ah, yes. Is the cost justified? That would of course depend upon the worthiness of the project, on how much you yourself are worth." He held up an index finger. "Consider this: what if every other person you have met on this programme was an actor, an agent of the programme designed to guide you along the path from nihilism to full rehabilitation? What if every structure, every encounter, was designed to bring you, and you alone, back from the brink of self-destruction to the healthy citizen you are becoming? What would that say about how much we value you?"

I exhaled slowly. "A lot. More than I can say."

"And if you were not the only one? If all the other participants were also being brought back from such a fate, being transformed from deathward to lifeward, would that diminish your value?"

"Perhaps a little, but it would still be a great deal."

The professor nodded with a slight smile.

"And would you prefer to live in a society that values even its outcasts that highly, or one that would simply have them destroyed or abandoned?"

"Purely out of self-interest, of course the former, but am I really worth that much?"

"If you are just a clump of cells, a brief pattern of atoms and nothing more, then of course not. If, on the other hand, you are an eternal soul, with more lasting value than every structure, institution, culture and world in existence today, then I'd say we have ourselves a bargain, wouldn't you?"

"I suppose so."

"If you are eternal, then what matters most is the character traits you are developing, the spiritual direction you are heading, far more than where you happen to be now, since the extrapolation into eternity will infinitely outweigh any possible starting point. No matter how low you have sunk, you always have a chance at redemption. No matter how high you have climbed, or been carried by others, at any point you may begin a downward slide. This is the greatest of all challenges, and the purpose of the programme, that through adventure and rediscovery of the great truths of life we may guide you onto a path of character growth."

Just as the professor was finishing a bell rang, signifying the end of the day's learning. The professor smiled. "Well, time has flown, hasn't it? But while we're on the subject of magnificence: after we have finished this text, and then looked at the question that is inscribed above our entrance from another angle, I will take you to get your first look at the city."

Chapter 13 – The City

In the gap between breakfast and the resumption of my classes the next morning, I went for a walk around the gardens. I passed many young couples with carved bone wedding necklaces, somewhere between a third and a half of the women in those couples were sporting rounded stomachs or pushing infants in carriages. We exchanged pleasantries, but did not engage in any extended conversation, as I was still mainly focused on exploring the grounds.

To my delight, as I neared the west cliff-face, I came across a little grove of disparity trees. I moved in among them and watched the changing patterns of colours as my image was gradually and increasingly fuzzily transferred from one tree to the next, alternating between negative and positive approximations of my appearance. I stepped in and out of the grove and tried to time how long my fading ghost images lasted.

Professor Brown passed by on his own morning walk through the gardens. He stopped and stood by my side. "Marvellous things, aren't they?"

"Yes, the first time I encountered one in the Wilderness Stage, I thought it was trying to communicate with me."

The Professor smiled. "You're not the first."

"I made a promise to find a good patch of soil to plant one of its seeds, but I lost that seed after coming through the tunnel."

"Well, one disparity tree seed is very much like another. When it is time for you to graduate, feel free to take a seed from here with you and plant it in your new home."

"Thank you, I think I'll do that. While we're on the subject of new life growing, I've come across a lot of women here that are either with child or newly mothers, yet none in the Wilderness Stage."

"That is a matter of policy. Whenever one of the women in the fortress becomes pregnant, we transport her and her husband directly to the Academy, since marriage and the raising of children is the foundation of civilization. The Wilderness Stage is no place for a child."

"What about the other tribes? Do pregnant women get transported to the Academy from them?"

"The women in the other tribes don't get pregnant; the food in the boxes is laced with contraceptives."

"Wow, that's a little harsh, isn't it?"

"Compared to all the other harshness in the valley? It's all part of the immaturity they live in back there, one more aspect of reality that they're sheltered from."

"I suppose so, but still ... there's so much to take in. I have a lot to learn, don't I?"

The professor smiled and nodded. "That you do, and you always will, just like the rest of us. Try considering it an opportunity rather than a burden."

He glanced down at his holoband. "And if I'm not mistaken, your next opportunity is in ten minutes."

On assembling in the morning a week later, we were taken from the Academy's main corridor through double doors to a long room that was empty other than a series of paintings along its walls. The professor met us there, then pointed his holoband at the end wall and wafted in front of it with his other hand.

Three sections split from the wall in front of us, the central one lifted into the ceiling and the two on either side slid away sideways. The opening led to a new corridor with crystalline walls into which delicate floral patterns had been engraved; they caught the light in slowly morphing rainbow patterns as we moved past them. Ahead of us were misted sparkling double doors engraved with trees, spirals and arches, which slid apart to reveal a great hallway with a vast bubble window facing us. Sunlight streamed through it, and beyond the window were all manner of buildings.

Great ornate arches, spiralling towers of silver, gold, green and blue, dominated by a cluster of what looked like massive coppery tree trunks with interlocking translucent blue crowns, all over a hundred metres high. Sleek vehicles of various shapes and colours slid through the air, most of them moving to and from the blue crowns, while others glided down in between the buildings in front of us.

"This is the city of Gateway, capital of Kalos, of the Chara system – our home."

"Wow, why couldn't we see any of this from the gardens, or from the Wilderness Stage?"

"There is a dome over the gardens that ensures no unauthorised access to the Academy, while also masking all traces of the city beyond, and the valley has high screens all around its edge for the same purpose. The screens there have less to do, since the Wilderness Stage is in an isolated location approximately one hundred kilometres away to the east, both to be far from urban influence and to save on the initial land purchase costs; you were brought here by underground train."

"So the cliffs around the gardens—"

"Are a completely unrelated rock formation. Though, to be fair, they did inspire the design of the Wilderness Stage.

"As I was saying, Kalos is the primary inhabited planet of the Chara system, the fifth of seven solar systems to have been colonised by man, though two other systems are being prepared for colony ships to arrive. The first robotic terraforming ships came here five hundred years ago, and the first colony ships made the sixty-year journey a century later. Our fastest vessels could theoretically travel back to Earth in fifty years, or to the nearest other colony in twenty, while signals transmitted via long-range quantum tunnelling take three months to reach the nearest colony. Of course, this is too long a delay for any sort of conversation, so we are largely independent of each other and keep each other informed of our progress via regular documentaries and research papers. Work is being done to reduce these times, but that is unlikely to affect any of us in the short term.

"Every one of these buildings you see is either occupied and functional, or open to the public to be explored. They may contain monuments and sculptures or incorporate such things into their architecture, but all are designed with a practical purpose in mind: recreation, education, entertainment, business, engineering, habitation, transport, most for a combination of such purposes. If you come to the window and look down, you may see a low star-shaped building with a central dome."

I moved up to the window and peered down over the dull coppery road along which sleek shapes sped. In front of the tree-like structures, and dwarfed by them, was what looked from this distance to be a small building in the shape of an eight-pointed star with a pale green central dome.

"That is where our elected representatives meet to discuss and implement any changes to our laws that need to be made. To be eligible for election to that office, you need to have been employed for at least a decade in some sort of business outside the legal profession, entertainment, the media or academia. Appointments are for five years, with no chance of re-election, and thanks to the Whittle Act of '24, all laws created must be written in plain language and whittled down to under 5,000 words. This all helps to create and maintain a set of laws that are clear, just, and in tune with the lives of ordinary citizens.

"All this we have built in four centuries, but it could easily have been different, and it can be lost. The greatest enemy of civilisation is not corruption or barbarianism, or suffering or even war, but complacency. Civilisations fall apart when their populations become lazy and apathetic, when they are content to merely drift through life and fail to value their own culture, fail to distinguish between the honourable and dishonourable, allow the corrupt to take over and the barbarians to loot and pillage unopposed.

"We need adventurers, visionaries and philosophers; explorers, innovators and entrepreneurs, people of wisdom and courage. We need the fresh perspective that you will provide, while honouring and appreciating all that our predecessors have discovered and achieved, and building upon the great foundation that they have laid for us. Are you up to the challenge?"

"We can help create something like this?" I gestured to the magnificent buildings.

"With co-operation, creativity and a lot of hard work, you'd be surprised how much we can achieve."

I nodded. "Help me prepare for what lies ahead, and I hope to make you proud." Several of the others nodded and murmured approvingly.

"That's the spirit. Now we will assess where your strengths lie, and then suggest various ways in which you can play to them. The final decision of course, will be yours."

We were taken separately through a series of rooms, each with different tasks to perform and puzzles to solve. Some made very little sense to me, others felt too easy. After we were finished and given our results (I was apparently gifted in engineering, problem solving and lateral thinking), a range of possible careers and career paths were suggested, each with an explanation of what kind of things it would involve. I made my initial target to work towards becoming a maintenance man for 4-D printers.

"Bear in mind that the career you choose now is not a life sentence. You may in the future develop other skills and interests that can be put to productive use, or notice new opportunities to work and improve the lives of those around you. Continue to educate yourselves and broaden your horizons. Never grow tired of learning, it is one of the greatest adventures of them all."

On my second day in the workshop, a tall man in blue overalls with broad shoulders, short red hair, a slightly crooked nose, and a friendly gleam in his green eyes walked up to me.

"Hello there, I heard you're studying to be a 4-D printer mechanic?"

"Yeah, that's my planned starting point."

"Finally! Gram and I have been looking for someone like you. I'm specialising in mining and extraction drones, Gram in mineral refiners; put the three together and we can build just about anything we want from scratch. We were thinking that once we graduate and get settled in, we could get together and build our own little moon base on Sidereos."

"Sounds like fun, but what about the power requirements?"

"Once we've earned enough, we can buy a compact thorium plant to start us off, then print a few more on-site as the power needs grow."

"Sounds like a plan, I'm in." I offered a hand. "Zephyr Walker."

"Excellent, Zephyr. Can I call you Zeph?"

"Yeah, why not?"

"OK, Zeph. I'm Bernard Puncheon, you can call me Bern, and that's Graham Lewis, or Gram." Bern gave a thumbs up to Gram, who was dressed in red overalls with narrower shoulders, tousled brown hair, a straight nose and pale brown eyes, and was working on a little contraption at a workbench across the room. He glanced up, clenched a celebratory fist, then resumed his work. "He'll introduce himself later, he's at a delicate stage with his project. You're fresh from the fortress, aren't you?"

"That's right, I came through just over a week ago, though I was only there a few days. How can you tell?"

"Oh, the engineers usually are. Which side of the river were you on?"

"The left side, if you're looking downstream."

"So was I. I devised a pipeline that supplied a waterfall by the river mouth for washing retrieved debris. Is that still working?"

"That was you? Wow, yes, it's still working very well. A fine piece of engineering."

"Thank you."

"I came up with an improved lifting mechanism that used water power instead of human power to lift things onto the plateau. I came through as soon as it was up and working."

"Excellent, I'm sure that will be a great help to them. How's Martin Grade?"

"Doing well, always friendly and helpful."

Bern smiled. "That's Martin all right. Did his beloved come back?"

"Beloved?"

He sighed and frowned. "Obviously not, then. He was about to be married to a lovely lady, but one of the other residents, who we called 'Stretch', wanted her for himself and tried to stop the wedding. He and Martin got into a fight, she tried to break it up and Stretch hit her with a punch he swung at Martin. She fell to the ground, hit her head on a sharp rock and disappeared. The elders of the fortress got together, judged and condemned Stretch to choose between being shot with arrows or jumping from a fortress tower. He jumped and disappeared, but Martin was inconsolable for days. He's

114

convinced she'll come back one day, and he'll win her heart again. There's no way he'd risk the tunnel before she comes back."

"That's awful. How long ago was that?

"Four months ago. I went through the tunnel a week or so afterwards, after I was sure Martin was going to be all right. I'm leaving some contact details with Professor Brown so he can get in contact with me when he graduates. Say hello to him for me if you see him before I do."

"I will."

Ѱ

Over the next few months, my classes went well and I spent ever more time in the libraries, engrossing myself in both technical books and classical literature as well as coordinating plans with Bern and Gram. Gram's hair was now a little less tousled, since he was getting to be on more than friendly terms with an aeroponics student in the lab next door by the name of Helen Stoner. Most evenings I found time to walk around the gardens and unwind.

I surprised some of my instructors with how quickly I grasped new concepts and was able to apply them in new ways. Pretty much all of them concurred that I had a promising future ahead of me, but then again maybe they said that to everyone.

When my graduation day came, I went back to the grove of disparity trees, took a single seed from one of them, wrapped it in a small plastic bag and placed it in my pocket.

A vaguely familiar voice behind me asked, "Hookless, is that you?"

I turned and could hardly believe my eyes.

"Queenie?"

She had a very different look about her. Calm and content, dressed elegantly in a long flowing dress with a piece of polished bone around her neck. She sighed and smiled with a small shake of the head. "It's Mary Grade now."

"I'm Zephyr Walker, literally 'Walker of the west wind' "

115

"So you're like the wind: unstoppable, uncatchable, unhookable? Maybe Hookless wasn't so far off." She smiled.

I smiled and nodded. "Maybe not. You made it all the way here. How did you get away from the Apples?"

"I used one of the beacons the Chief kept in the back of his cave."

"The Chief kept beacons? What a hypocrite."

"It's worse than that. He kept them for himself and the recruiters. As a recruiter, I was instructed to use the beacon to escape from any raid that got near the cave, then make my way back to the tribe after things calmed down. He'd done that himself a couple of times."

"So he knew all along, but told everyone in the tribe that they throw you back in the Gravity Ring? That's terrible."

"I only found that out once I was a recruiter. They told us the other tribes would tear us apart if they found us, and after all the tribal fighting I saw, who was I to doubt it? During the raid after I failed to recruit you, I was determined to escape far from the others when I activated the beacon. I found myself in a cave high up in the cliffs where there was a small stream and a box of food. I lasted up there for maybe a week before a tribe discovered me and I used the beacon to escape from them."

"So you reached the fortress, and you got married there ... wait, what did you say your name was?"

"Mary Grade."

"You m-married Martin Grade?"

She smiled. "Oh, he's such a sweet man, and so good to me. It's hard to believe he still wanted me after all I did for the Apples."

Does she know? Should I mention it?

"So you took the tunnel together?"

She patted her stomach lovingly, and I noticed that it was slightly rounded.

"No, it's all thanks to this little fellow. One of the wilderness wardens told me I was expecting a baby, and then they took Martin and me up onto the cliffs, through the screen then down into a capsule that took us here. It was quite a ride."

"Congratulations, that sounds a lot more pleasant than the tunnel. So how long ago did you arrive, Quee—I mean, Mary?"

"This morning, there's so much here, a lot to take in."

"That's an understatement if ever I heard one." I said with a smile.

My holoband chimed a gentle chorus.

"Oh, no. Talk about bad timing, grr. I wish I could stay and catch up with all we've both been up to, but I graduate in half an hour. I've got to go and get ready, and then I won't be back here at all."

"Oh no, that's not fair. We've got so much to talk about."

"I'll talk to Professor Brown about passing on some contact details to you, so you can get in touch with me as soon as you get through the programme here. Martin was a good friend of mine."

"They can do that?"

"Lots of people do it, it's no problem at all."

"That sounds good. Good luck with your graduation."

"Thank you. Say hello to Martin for me and for Bernard Puncheon, who's already out in the city. Don't forget to get in touch once you graduate."

"I will and we won't."

⚘

The hall where we got our first glimpse of the city was set up with rows of chairs and a stage under the great window. All that month's graduates sat in the front two rows of twenty chairs, behind us sat three rows of instructors and other Academy staff, and to one side of the stage was a choir in purple robes. One stepped forward and began a solo, the others joining in with additional voices as the song progressed, building to a magnificent five-part harmony, then narrowing back down to a solo for the final verse:

'Twas through falling that I found my feet,
Through wandering my way;
Through lostness where my soul belongs,
Through night I found the day.

Through anarchy what order means,
Through suffering my healing;
Through loneliness my greatest friend,
Through numbness all new feeling.

Through dying to that world of lies,
I found the living truth I sought;
A nomad's path has brought me home,
To gain the good that can't be bought.

Each morning is now fresh and new,
Each glimpse of beauty treasured;
Each moment with my one great love
Worth more than can be measured.

Every kindly act I see
Will be appreciated
As heaven's touch upon the world,
And all that was created.

As the audience applauded the choir, Professor Brown stood from his seat and walked to the centre of the stage.

"This is the anthem of the Academy. It was written by Alison Swann, one of the first graduates of the programme. She went on to become one of this planet's greatest songwriters and helped the outside world see how valuable this programme is.

"Now it is your turn. You have been given a solid foundation, it is up to you all to build upon it. Continue working hard, continue learning, continue creating. Explore, experiment and excel in your chosen fields. Look around you for unmet needs, unused resources and new opportunities. Go show the world that you are worth the investment made in you."

The audience applauded us as we received our graduation certificates, then began to disperse and we gathered around the professor.

"Do you think we could meet Mrs Swann?" I asked.

"I'm afraid not, she passed on, eight years ago."

"Oh, I'm sorry to hear that."

"Don't be, she enjoyed a long and fruitful life, living to see her twentieth great-grandchild before she died at the age of ninety-eight."

"Ninety-eight? How long has this programme been running?"

"A little over seventy years."

"That long? How have you kept going?"

"It was started by donations from like-minded individuals, and still has external supporters, but is now chiefly sustained by contributions from graduates from the programme. Contributions are entirely voluntary, and you may opt out at any time, but many choose to send us three to five per cent of their income, and that has been more than enough to sustain us."

"That little?"

"This class was on the small side, we average just over ten graduates per week, who go on to lead productive lives for another forty years or more, about half of those supporting us at any one time. This currently works out at over twelve thousand highly educated, highly motivated people supporting our efforts here, enabling us to do all that we do now. Would you like to become one of them?"

Most of us nodded.

"Thank you. If you head over to the booth by the door over there, we will set that up with your new employers. Your earnings may be meagre to start with, but every little helps and you have all shown yourselves to be highly capable students; in time, I am sure that your capacity to contribute value to others will grow far beyond what it is now. Do me proud."

The crowd shook hands with the professor, thanking him and the rest of the staff for all of their efforts, then dispersed towards the booth or their individual instructors to say their goodbyes.

I lingered until the last of them was gone, then leant towards the professor and quietly asked, "Do you think I'll ever run into someone who knew me from before I was sent here, who'll know me by my old name?"

"Five hundred million people live on this planet, ten million in this city alone, so unless you were some sort of major celebrity, the chances of that happening are very remote. Even so, I wouldn't recommend seeking out your old life. Whoever you were, whatever friends or environment you were exposed to, something led to choices that ruined your life, or the lives of those around you.

"For now, go out into the world. Work hard, discover new things and enjoy yourself."

"Thank you. I will." I said, taking up my suitcases and moving on to the booth, then the waiting transport.

Chapter 14 – Urban Life

The side of the transport bloomed open, then closed around me. I sat down and the vehicle soared up into the air, relaxing melodies played as it left the opulent buildings behind. It took me far away to a set of low-rise cylindrical buildings dotted around a park, which was enclosed in a translucent-green ring decorated with images of mountain ranges, complex mechanical wonders, fountains, forests and romantic castles. Nearby were multiple small domes, which functioned as storage vats and warehouses for raw materials, and next to them collection points for broken machines and used construction materials, where the latter could be sorted and reprocessed into the former.

My flat in one of the low-rise buildings was pleasant enough, and the food printer gave a nice variety of meals, but neither was quite up to the standard of what I'd been provided with in the Academy. I wasn't complaining; the sense of freedom, of my own place, more than made up for any shortcomings, and it was all palatial compared to life in the wilderness valley.

I turned up for work in the morning with ten minutes to spare, meeting my new boss at the door as he arrived. He looked to be a man in his late fifties, wearing a red and grey jumpsuit and a blue cap that like his features showed signs of wear. The sharp hazel eyes either side of his bulbous nose quickly appraised me and shone with mirth and wisdom. He had a slightly poetic lilt to his voice.

"Punctuality, I like that." He nodded and gave me a fatherly smile. "Right, here's the deal. You're on probation for a month, where you'll travel with and assist me. If I like you and things are working well, you'll become my apprentice for a year, then an employee for another two. What happens after that will be entirely up to you. What do you say?" He offered a hand.

"Sounds good to me." I nodded and shook his hand.

"OK, Mr Walker. The name's Patrick Marley, but you can call me Pat, like everyone else."

"Thank you, Pat. My friends call me 'Zeph'."

"Right you are, then, Zeph. Let's start by showing you all the tools we'll be using. You let me know if any of them are any different to what you had up at the Academy ..."

⚜

We went around a pleasant leafy housing estate, fixing robotic cleaners and 4-D printers (and doing other minor chores) mostly for pleasant old ladies and retired couples. They were very appreciative of our work, offered us home-made cupcakes and other treats by the trayful. After I'd unblocked a drain and replaced a kitchen tap for a silver-haired old lady, she turned to Patrick with a mischievous glint in her pale blue eyes and spoke with a similar lilt.

"Well, Pat, I must compliment you on your new assistant – a very nice and well-mannered young man, he is. If my girls weren't all happily married, I'd be making some introductions."

Pat smiled and punched me in the shoulder. "Now there's an appraisal to be proud of. He's from the Programme, Mrs. Minter."

"Oh, like Miss Swann? They do such good work, don't they? So then, Mr Walker, what do you make of our little city?"

"It's amazing, beautiful. So much to explore and discover – I hardly know where to begin."

"Oh, to be young again and see the world with fresh eyes. What a privilege, what an adventure!"

"It is, and one I am grateful for."

"That's the spirit! Best of luck to you."

"Thank you, Mrs. Minter, you're too kind."

It was an enjoyable time, and I really felt like I was doing some good. Not the most lucrative work, but very rewarding.

The next day the majority of our clients were young families with preschool children. Little boys watched us work with wide-eyed fascination, as if we were heroes battling monsters in their homes. Patrick always found a way to occupy our little audience by having them hold a tool for him or giving them a series of little pegs to bash into a grid with a plastic hammer, making sure to loudly admire their handiwork.

Interspersed with these were the homes of professionals with no children, where the pay was a little better but we just went in and got the job done as quietly as possible while the client was in another room.

Most of my evenings would be taken up with studying, learning all I could about mechanics, astronomy, robotics and programming. At the end of the second week as I returned to my flat and was considering getting in contact with Bern and Gram about the moon base project, I found a number of paper advertisements had been stuffed in my letter box. I thought it strange, given the propensity for using holobands for all communication, but had to admit the feel of paper in my hand was somehow reassuring.

Included in the pile was a red-orange advert for a pizza place, at the bottom of which was a barcode for a free sample. My holoband detected the barcode and highlighted it on the page, asking *Activate single-use 4-D printer barcode from Luigi's Pizza Emporium? Code verified by Dillweaver Food Safety Lab.*

"Why not? Activate code."

Downloading recipe, linking to 4-D printer.

A green indicator lit up on my printer, then flashed orange.

Warning, your printer has insufficient resolution for this recipe. Download alternative recipe?

"Oh, I guess I don't have the latest model. Fine, download alternative."

The light switched back to green, flashed for a few seconds, then went back to a steady light.

Various hums, whirs and the occasional gentle hiss could be heard from the machine and *Preparing Recipe* appeared below the light for about thirty seconds, then the door opened to reveal a five-centimetre square piece of thick-crust ham and pineapple pizza with perfectly browned cheese. I took it out and took a bite, nodding.

"Pretty good."

A male voice with what I presumed was an Italian accent declared from my holoband, "Hey, now, she's only a taste. If you wanna the real ting, come to Luigi's. You got it?"

"I might just do that." I smiled, turned the paper over for a list of the nearest outlets, and my jaw dropped. Across it was scrawled in a thick black pen:

If you want a memory refresh, come to the branch on Stowell Street and ask for a private table. Once there, order the Margherita Special. No credit, bring an untraceable high-value consumable to pay for it.

I glanced all around me, my pulse racing, then rushed over to the window and looked for anything out of place, someone or something loitering, watching me. Being unfamiliar with how my surroundings were supposed to look made it a hopeless task; the fact that nothing stood out to me was hardly reassuring.

How did they know? How did they find me? Did they follow me from the Academy, or get my address some other way?

I took some deep breaths and attempted to calm myself down.

How much of a secret is it that I'm from the Academy, anyway? No one seems to mind. Could this be part of the Programme, a test, or a genuine offer?

I slumped down into the nearest armchair, paper in hand.

This life is going well, but a chance to discover who I was ... can I really turn that down? That old life destroyed me, and who knows what else on the way down, would it destroy me again? Would I be able to make amends, heal old wounds or get dragged down into a life of crime?

How can I make that choice?

How can I not?

I went down to the nearest boutique and bought an expensive bottle of wine, then took a transport to Stowell Street. My fellow passengers included tired-looking mothers with small children, teenage boys and girls engrossed in their holobands (or in each other), senior citizens of all stripes and demeanours, and various adults with inscrutable expressions.

Did someone here send me that note? Are any of these people following me?

I instinctively gripped my shoulder bag a little tighter as we approached the Stowell Street stop, and my suspicions were not eased when ten others exited with me and dispersed in various directions. The buildings here were terraced with mostly oriental flourishes to them, but showed considerable signs of wear; this was obviously not the most prestigious part of town.

The street lighting was intermittent, and dim alleyways intimidated me with their gaping maws as I walked past. I approached the warmer and more brightly lit pizza establishment, which exuded all sorts of delicious aromas to draw me in and make my mouth water.

Most of the patrons of this place wore long coats despite the warm weather, multiplying my doubts about the wisdom of coming here, but I urged myself though that mental barrier – the lure of my past was too strong. Occasional boisterous bursts of laughter and drunken ramblings from one corner or the other drowned out the otherwise muted conversation at most of the tables, which were circular and covered with tablecloths made from interwoven red, white and green ribbons. Ahead of me was the counter, above which were pictures of delicious-looking pizzas cooked to perfection alongside exotic multi-coloured salads, and lists of unfamiliar dishes down each wall.

A man by the door wearing a red, white and green striped shirt and a nametag in the shape of a pizza slice that read *Brian* inclined his head towards me. "Can I help you, sir?"

"Um, yes," I answered quietly. "I'd like a private table, please."

"Certainly, sir. This way, please."

I noticed another man in a similar uniform take Brian's place as I followed him through a door to the side, leading to a corridor with several wooden doors in it, each with just a single number on it.

Door number five was opened for me, revealing a small room with no windows, luxuriously padded benches along a rectangular table and low, romantic lighting. Brian closed the door behind us and gestured to the leather-bound menus on the table.

"Can I get you something to drink, sir, while you decide on your order?"

"I, I'm here for the Margherita Special."

He inclined his head slightly in acknowledgement, but there was no surprise in his voice.

"I see. Your name, sir?"

"Zephyr Walker."

"And did you bring something with you?"

I opened my bag and retrieved the bottle of wine.

"Thank you." He scanned the bottle's label with his holoband, then nodded.

"Yes, that will do. Please come with me."

Brian led me back through door number five into the main corridor, then through a door in the opposite wall marked *STAFF ONLY*.

Ahead of us was a corridor leading to the kitchens, to the left and right a series of doors leading to store rooms. We took the first door on the right, into a small walk-in cupboard full of cleaning supplies, with several brooms, mops and dustpans and brushes hanging from hooks on the far wall.

"You still use these things?"

He shrugged. "Whenever the robotic cleaners break down." He stepped on a barely discernible square in the back right corner of the room and pushed on the wall, which swung back to reveal an utterly empty ashen-walled space that was perhaps a metre wide and two deep.

"Step inside, please, and hold onto the rail. My colleague will take you from here."

I walked past the panel, which was closed behind me, and a light switched on, revealing a plastic handrail on the far wall that was a darker shade of cinereal. I reached out and held onto it, then felt the floor shift slightly as the cubicle descended. I looked up at the back of the panel and saw it rising up away from me at a speed that smoothly increased to a metre or two per second before disappearing past the ceiling. I felt a lightness that indicated a continued steady increase in speed, but the wall opposite me was utterly featureless, so it was difficult to judge how deep I was going. Three or four seconds later the lightness switched to a more pronounced heaviness as the lift came to a controlled stop at a silvery door.

It opened outwards into a large oval space with a domed ceiling, dominated by what appeared to be a large high-tech throne, complete with a step up to the reclining chair in a tubular metal frame. There was a bulky rectangular shape on its left side, a standard desk and workstation on the right, and a bulbous grey dome overhead. A technician in a less-than-pristine lab coat with a swarthy complexion and dark brown curly hair sat at the workstation, and looked to be making some sort of adjustments to the device.

Another man in a slightly worn lab coat, who could have been the technician's twin brother stood by the door and gestured towards the contraption with a bow of the head.

"Good evening, Mr Walker. Please take a seat."

I took a few deep breaths as I moved slowly towards the imposing machine.

"Now, don't worry, the important thing is to relax and remain still once you're seated, so we can get as good an image of what they did as possible. We'd prefer to do this part without needing sedatives."

Sedatives?

I gave a nervous laugh. "OK, you do realize that what you're telling me isn't helping me to calm down."

"Of course, my apologies. When you've done this hundreds of times, you tend to forget what it's like to be here for the first time. Everything is going to be all right, you're in safe hands. Just sit down, relax, and let us take a look. We can't read your mind, if that's what you're worried about. We'll just be looking at what kind of memory wipe you were given, so we can know how to counter it."

"Thank you, that's better, but before I do, could I ask how you knew to specifically target me with your advertisement?"

"The same way we find anyone; we have people watching out for graduates from the Programme, occasionally our sponsors will tell us about someone we missed."

"You have sponsors?"

"What, did you think a single bottle of wine would cover our costs? It helps, but the brunt of our expenses are covered by people who appreciate what we do, including our former clients. We don't insist on it, but if things turn out well for you, you might want to remember us. A little gratitude goes a long way, you know?"

"All right, I understand. OK." I took another couple of deep breaths and then sat in the chair. Its cushioning was soft, but supportive.

"If you need to shift the position of your head to be comfortable, then please do that now. Otherwise, we'll begin."

"No, this is fine."

A button was pressed and a padded strap wrapped around my forehead, holding me softly but firmly in place. The bulbous dome descended and tilted until my entire head was surrounded, though I could still see out through a notch in its front. There was an almost imperceptible hum, and there was a mild prickling sensation at the base of my skull, which spread and grew in intensity until it felt like my skull was peeling away completely, leaving my brain utterly exposed. It wasn't painful, it was as if my mind was expanding to an infinite dark horizon in every direction, though I was still aware of my surroundings.

The sensation eased and I noticed the technician with his hands in the air, manipulating an image in front of his monitor that was invisible to me with a furrowed brow, then looking at me with suspicion, alternating concerned glances between me and whatever the display was showing. He then beckoned to the man at the door.

"Jim, come over here and take a look at this."

Jim walked over to the workstation. The technician pressed a button and Jim started.

"Wow."

"When did you last see something like that?"

"Not in a long time. That's going to be tricky."

"Could you please tell me what's going on?" I asked with another nervous laugh. "You're not really filling me with a lot of confidence, here."

"Oh, don't worry, it's not dangerous or anything, just unusual."

"What is?"

"What they did to your memory. It's not the usual blanket dampening, but a very precise pattern wipe. Whoever did this clearly valued your mental skills, they've done all they can to leave those as untouched as possible while clearing all your personal memories."

"They valued my mental skills? What does that mean? That I was some sort of criminal mastermind?"

"I don't know. It could be a lot of things. Like I said, we can't read your mind, or your old memories. It's just that the type of memory wipe you had is going to make it much more difficult to recover what was cleared. I think the best we can hope for is to reawaken some of the peripheral impressions at the edges of the pattern. That's mostly going to manifest itself as faint remnants of what your life was like before: feelings of déjà vu, uneasiness around those you previously had conflicts with, subconscious things – affecting your dreams more than anything else. I'm sorry to disappoint you, but that's all we can do. Shall we?"

"That is disappointing, yes." I sighed. "But it's better than nothing. Do what you can."

The prickling sensation returned, as did the dark horizon, except this time I sensed distant pinpricks of light growing imperceptibly slowly, though I somehow knew they were massive objects rushing towards me at incredible speeds from unimaginable distances. As they grew closer, the lights became blurry, as did my normal vision.

The room began to spin and I found myself struggling to keep my eyes open. My struggles were in vain, and soon everything went black …

ψ

I opened my eyes, and my head was pounding. I could smell alcohol on my clothes and my surroundings felt like they were swimming, which turned out to be the back of a small transport.

"Where am I?" I asked with slurred speech.

"On your way home after passing out in the pleasure district. Must have been quite a night."

I rubbed my eyes and my temples. "I suppose it was."

"I don't know why people would do that to themselves. I mean, it might be fun at the time, but then you can't remember anything afterwards. What's the point of having a good time if you have no memories at the end of it?"

I half smiled. "You might have a point there. I was hoping for a few good memories from this one."

Chapter 15 – Memory Fragments

Getting home was something of a blur, I assume the cabbie helped me up to my flat and I somehow made my way to the sofa before giving in to weariness. My dreams were fitful and strange, odd shapes and symbols swirling around me, falling past blurred faces, some filling me with dread, others with a sense of belonging.

I awoke somewhat rested, glad that today was my day off, and drew what I could remember of my dream in a sketching application on my holoband. I checked my credit level, I still had more than eighty left, which should be more than enough for this week's food, plus a nice little sum left over.

There were just under twelve hours of daylight left, and my flat was towards the outskirts of the city, so I called up the urban multi-stop transport route map and found a route that had a stop four hundred metres from my door, going into the centre and all the way to the very edge of the city on the other side.

A return ticket wouldn't use up too much of my budget, but the chances of finding something familiar on just that one line were probably not that high, so maybe a better bet would be to buy a one-way ticket, then come back via one of the semi-circular routes that travelled through many different districts. That would cost a lot, meaning I'd have to skimp on food for the next week, but even the cheap options were luxuries compared to what I had been eating in the valley. An all-day travel pass would give me a lot more flexibility, but was out of my price range. I could wait another week and save up a little more, but these new memories might fade by then, and I'd miss my chance to take advantage of them altogether.

The next transport would be coming through in fifteen minutes, so I quickly printed a few of the cheapest sandwiches on the printer's pre-set menu, filled a couple of water bottles and put them all in a shoulder bag before locking up the flat and running for the stop. I made it with three minutes to spare.

On the journey into town I saw a lot of things I remembered from my journey out from the Academy, but nothing that jumped out at me. Once past the gigantic tree structures and spiralling towers, we passed fascinating buildings of all shapes and sizes; edifices topped with square, pentagonal, hexagonal and octagonal pyramids, even some constructed of half-buried inverted pyramids that merged together into one floor and continued upwards in various ways.

There were oval-budded columns, complete with transparent leaves and petals in places; there were flattened, rounded and pointed arches and domes; structures based on tapering quadruple, sextuple or octuple helices, some that arched over and dove into central spires, others that stood alone and proud. Whenever we got close enough to a building, I could see that their forms weren't smooth, but in fact engraved or painted with all sorts of subtle patterns. No one building was quite like another, but none of their shapes matched the ones in my dream.

In between the buildings were large paved areas decorated with trees, fountains, lights, sculptures, small public gardens and little market stalls. Here and there were small crowds gathered around street performers of one type or another. Many people walked, while others scooted around individually or in pairs on little, wheeled vehicles. It was a vibrant place.

Further on out of the city, the buildings were smaller and less ornate, the spaces between a little less crowded and broken up with larger areas of greenery, including several connected parks. As we approached the end of the line, the buildings were similar in design to the low-rise buildings I lived in. Beyond that were small individual houses with fenced-in gardens, uniform in their basic structures, but with their own individual touches and extensions. Children ran and played in the road between the houses, and the transport did not take off this time, instead extending wheels from its floor and trundling along the road for the last five stops of its route.

The last stop was perhaps a hundred meters short of the last row of houses. I got out and breathed in the sweet fresh air that blew in

133

from the fields past the housing estate, though there were other scents here, too: apple and cherry blossom from trees in some of the gardens, fresh-cut grass and the mouth-watering smell of a barbeque being held nearby. Dogs barked, children laughed and played, and a mottled cat sunned itself on the top of a wall to my right; the muffled sounds of whirring tools indicated work being done in workshops or gardens nearby.

I walked over to the gate at the end of the estate and looked out at the world beyond the city. Gently wafting fields of grain, rolling hills around a lake and snow-capped mountains beyond them, terrain that just invited you out to explore and discover. I turned and leant against the gatepost, taking in the suburban activity all around me.

Now this is a good life. Once I earn enough, maybe I could move out to a place like this. If I learn nothing else today, I'll at least have a new goal in mind.

I looked at my holoband and found I had eight hours of daylight remaining. The transport had already left without me, the next one would be in half an hour, but the next circular transport would be in twenty-five minutes. I got out a water bottle, drank half of it, then started jogging back the three kilometres to where the circular route crossed the one I had taken.

The going was easy and the day was pleasant, though some clouds were gathering and it started to rain shortly before I arrived back at my desired stop, starting out as a light drizzle, with the raindrops growing in size as I approached the shelter, hammering its transparent roof with a somehow soothing clatter once I got inside and shook the moisture from my hair, to the mild amusement of some of the others waiting there.

The transport arrived. I paid my fare and sat down in the only available window seat, though its walls on both sides were entirely transparent from the inside, so all the seats had much the same view of the outside.

The buildings around us were about half the size of the smaller ones in the centre – around ten or twelve storeys high – each district that we passed through had its own distinct architectural style, with individual buildings having touches and colour schemes to distinguish them from each other.

The first district was mostly comprised of smooth glassy towers, the second had mainly Georgian-style buildings, the third Romanesque, the fourth Chinese and the fifth had Renaissance elements (at least that's what my holoband was telling me as we passed them). All I could tell was that they had a different feel to them and each had their charms, but still nothing stood out to me. I munched on a sandwich as I watched the skyline go by.

Maybe I never lived in this city. Maybe I've been wasting my time and money on this. No, I wouldn't say waste, I've seen a lot of things that would be worth taking a closer look at on another day, and I'll be within walking distance of home in another half an hour. It's been a good trip.

As we reached a sixth gradual change in styles (I hadn't had time to look up what it was), my vision briefly flashed completely dark with a rainbow-coloured lightning bolt down the middle in an unusual shape. As my normal vision returned, I saw that the path of the coloured lightning closely matched the outline of a passing tower.

Wait, was that from my dream? Do I know this tower?

I hurriedly brought up the sketching app and scrolled through my drawings. Yes, there was the outline, or something similar. I twisted around in my seat to look back at the tower, but we had gone around a corner and it was already behind other buildings. As I twisted, I felt my elbow bump into someone's arm and heard something clatter onto the floor. I looked up to see an old lady looking forlornly down at a transparent box containing a brightly coloured cylindrical object with floral shapes on top of it.

"I'm terribly sorry, I really didn't mean to do that. I just need to get …"

"That was a birthday cake for my granddaughter," she informed me, as the transport came to a stop and people began filing out, while those who stayed where they were gave me disapproving glares. I felt like I wanted to shrivel into a small heap and disappear. I slithered down from my chair and reached for the box, bringing it back up as gently as I could as other people got into the transport and it started up again.

"Is it going to be all right?"

She eyed the cake from various angles.

"The flowers on this side are a little squashed and the icing is cracked here, but with a little work it can be fixed."

I spent the next two or three stops asking about the granddaughter, getting to know Gladys, offering my contact details and promising all sorts of future help until the other passengers no longer looked at me like I was the embodiment of all that was wrong with the world. I finally bid my warm farewells and disembarked, looking back the way the transport had come and consulting the route map on my holoband to try and work out where I had seen that tower. Unfortunately the route had zigzagged between buildings, and I had lost count of how many turns it had made or stops it had taken. I jogged back the way the route had been flown, skirting around flower beds and statues, watching the sky for the distinctive shape, but these buildings were all quite similar.

Is that it? Could be ... no, that edge of the building is a little too wavy, isn't it? That one is more like it, but shouldn't it be on the other side of the route? Let's try that other one further down, those white spheres under each balcony sort of feel right ...

I came up to the third building, which was a green glassy tower subtly shaped like a series of cresting waves, and approached the doors. The forms of billowing sails were engraved in the main entrance's crystalline double doors. It was vaguely familiar, but nowhere near the spark of the outline. I looked around the area. *Am I missing something?*

I took a few steps further back and looked around. The tower to my right was almost the same as the one before me: they were a pair of towers with a bridge between them two-thirds of the way up, shaped like a breaking wave forming a tunnel. I walked over to the second tower, and there was another flash of coloured lightning.

The tower's oval crystal doors were engraved with a profile depicting the rays of the setting sun, and the way the light caught that profile as it crossed the edge of the doors matched another shape from my dream, even producing the same rainbow of colours.

Wow. This must be it. Where am I? What was this place to me?

A large bronze plaque above the door read *SUNSET SURF TOWER.*

To the right of the doors was a list of names, each on their own bronze plate. There didn't seem to be any company headquarters here, it was apparently just a residential block. None of the names sparked any memories, but from what I gathered, they specifically wiped names from our memories, so maybe that didn't mean much.

Did I live here, or someone I knew?

I looked around at the people milling past, none of them seemed familiar, and none seemed to react to my presence, not even the ones going into and out of the building. There was a raised flower bed a little way from the entrance, I decided to sit there in full view of people making for the building entrance, eat my last sandwich and wait for someone to notice me.

People went past of all shapes, sizes and colours: some walking alone with a look of determination or disappointment, relaxed couples on a stroll through the area, people nervously walking their dogs, or chattering away in groups.

Am I somehow invisible, or so unremarkable that people don't notice me? Is this a bad place to sit?

Time passed, I shifted from seat to seat, and occasionally someone would glance my way then carry on, with no signs of recognition. My legs grew a little stiff, I stood, stretched and walked a few laps around the flower bed before sitting down again and drinking the last of my water. This earned me a few quizzical looks from passers-by, but no more than that.

Hours passed, the sun got a little lower in the sky and I began to plan my route home on my holoband.

It's been a good day all told, this place is obviously important somehow, and only five kilometres from my flat, I can walk that next time and save myself some mon—

There was a sound of breaking glass to my right. I turned my head and saw a beautiful woman who had dropped both of her bags of shopping and was staring at me with an open mouth.

"You … came back …"

To call her beautiful was an understatement; she had deep dark brown eyes to get lost in, elegant, yet approachable features framed with two curtains of curly dark auburn hair. She had a fine figure and a posture that somehow simultaneously radiated neediness and strength, vulnerability and resilience, wisdom and otherworldliness. My spirit spread its wings and I had a sudden urge to rush over and wrap her up in my arms, to never let her go again …

And then she burst into tears and stood there sobbing.

I felt my spirit plunge from the sky and hit the ground like a stone gargoyle knocked off the top of one of the buildings around us.

Was this my crime? Did I obsess over and stalk this beautiful creature, then do terrible things to her once she was in my grasp? What kind of despicable man was I?

A burly man in a broad-brimmed hat and trench coat saw what was going on and stood between us, eyeing me suspiciously.

"Is this man bothering you, miss?"

I picked up my bag and slowly backed away.

"If I hurt you in the past, then I'm really sorry. I'll just be leaving now."

"No, you fool!" she shouted, pushing past the burly man, then ran over to me and wrapped her arms around me.

"I was your wife."

Chapter 16 – Introductions

I stood there motionless for a while, not knowing what to do or say.

"Wha- my wife?"

"Mmhmm." She nodded without letting go of me. I slowly opened my arms and placed them around her, at any moment expecting her to explode in outrage at my forwardness, but instead she squeezed me even tighter to herself and purred, "Mmm, I've missed you so much."

I shook my head, trying to process all of this. "My wife. Wow, are you sure?"

She drew her head back and looked at me with a raised eyebrow. "You think I throw myself at strangers in the street and tell them we were married?"

"No, ah, I mean, this is just a lot to take in, you know? There's this whole other life I wish I knew about. I'm so sorry I let you down, I—"

She placed a finger on my lips, looking into my eyes with deep concern. "No, no, no. You didn't, not at all, you made it all the way back here."

"But I must have let you down enormously, to get thrown in the—"

"Shh, it's all right, it's all right, but let's not talk about it here. Come inside, up to our apartment."

I looked up at the tower. "We lived here? That would explain it."

"You remember?"

"Just some shapes, outlines, vague impressions without their context. The profile of the tower, the way the light catches those doors. When I first saw you, I had a really strong urge to wrap my arms around you."

She smiled. "Ooh, we can definitely work with that last one."

"Heh." I smiled and held her a little tighter, then glanced up at what she'd dropped and grimaced. "Those bags don't look so promising, though."

She turned to see the one on the right leaking red fluid and sighed. "Oh, that's not good. There's broken glass in there now."

"Maybe we can salvage something."

I went over to the bag and opened it up. Fresh carrots at the top, some sort of meat in a plastic packet below that, then what I assumed was a kind of bread, with the broken bottle of wine at the bottom. "That's a lot of fresh ingredients. Why don't you get your printer to make it? It's a lot cheaper, isn't it?"

"They taste different, and some people are picky."

"I'm sorry, I didn't mean it as an insult."

"Don't worry about it, what's important is that you're here now."

I emptied the sandwich wrappings from my shoulder bag into the nearest bin and carefully lifted the carrots and meat from the damaged plastic bag, placing them in my shoulder bag. I then slowly lifted the plastic bag at arm's length as it continued to drip precious red fluid onto the pavement and carefully dropped it into the same bin. "I'm not sure there's much more I can do."

"The street cleaning machines can cope with the rest, just come on in."

I picked up the other bag of shopping and she led me through the crystal doors, which glided open gracefully. We moved towards a row of four pairs of silvery doors, each etched with a different marine scene. The second pair on the left opened as we approached and we stepped inside. The doors closed and I felt us being whisked upwards.

"Are you sure about this? I don't even know your name."

She looked up at me with misty eyes. "Eleanor Elizabeth Charter, you called me Ellie C."

"Wow, that's a nice name. What was mine?"

"Steven Arnold Charter. You made a leaflet for a special offer to upgrade from Ellie B to Ellie C, put it on my desk, then got the ring out while I was reading it." She smiled, staring into space, then looked up at me again. "My maiden name was Bourne."

"You kept my name?"

"Well, legally I'm your widow; the programme has confused things there a little. What's your name now?"

"Zephyr Walker. Walker to remind me to persevere through all difficulties, Zephyr to remind me of what I used to be, just a rider on the wind."

"Zephyr … Zephyr," she repeated, as if tasting the word. "It sounds, exotic. Distinguished. Even romantic. I mean, I like it, but it's going to take some getting used to."

I smiled. "I've been saying that myself a lot recently; it's nice to hear it from someone else for a change." My smile dropped as a thought occurred to me. "Hmm, now that I come to think of it, I'm surprised they released me in the same city as you, if they didn't want me to recover my old life."

"This is a big place, and they only have one academy; everyone is released here."

"Then I'm lucky I lived here in the first place."

"You worked hard to get here from a village half a megam away."

"Five hundred kilometres isn't that far."

"Maybe not geographically, but it's a big jump financially."

The silver doors opened into a small corridor, carpeted with a rippling blue-green pattern and walls painted with a long image of amber-tinged clouds against a pale blue sky. The little screen by the doors indicated that this was the tenth floor.

Ellie stepped out of the lift and turned to the left, then beckoned to me with a smile.

"This way."

She stopped at an orange door and hopped up and down, giggling with excitement.

"I've waited so long for this."

I sighed. *What if I'm a big disappointment?*

142

She gestured into her holoband and the door slid open. The flat seemed to contradict itself; it had beautiful tiled floors and ornate and stylish built-in furnishings, but with glaring bare patches of wall all over the place, and the free-standing furniture was sparse and rudimentary. The layout was dominated by a large open space lit from above by what appeared to be daylight, in the middle of which stood a plastic set of table and chairs that looked even cheaper than the ones back in my flat.

"Is this the top floor?"

"What? Oh, you mean the light, no, that's just from the garden floor above."

People can see down into here from the garden? You don't worry about that?

"It's our own private garden, so no."

"The flat comes with its own garden?"

"Oh yes, the stairs up to it are over there."

"We must have been rich."

"It took a lot of work to afford it, it was a big improvement on where we started. After your conviction, I had to sell our transport as well as most of the removable fixtures and artwork in here, but I couldn't bear the thought of losing this place."

"I can understand that." I said, taking it all in.

"I'm afraid the sofa and armchairs were the first to go, together with the wallscreen."

"But you've got a sofa, over there."

"Oh, that? I just printed and assembled a simple plastic bench, then cut a cheap mattress in half lengthways and sewed it into a fabric cover that hooks over the back of the bench."

"That's a good idea, and looks like you did a good job, too."

"Thank you, but you really should have seen our old one."

"Look, it's fine. It makes this place seem more real, less intimidating, if you know what I mean."

She tilted her head to the slide a little and gave a warm half-smile. "Um, I think I do. It's very nice of you to say that."

"It's just the truth. All of this has been a lot to take in. If this was a palace full of luxuries it would be even weirder, less relatable, you know?"

"I understand." She placed a hand on mine, it felt warm and reassuring, so right and yet …

"Shall I put these things away?"

"Oh, right, the fridge is over here." Again it was a simple white box with shelves, bottom-of-the-range model, sparsely stacked.

"I'm sorry everything is so basic."

"Are you kidding? In the Wilderness Stage, I slept on a bag of straw in a house made of grass, sticks and mud, and that was luxury. All this, I still can't get over how amazing all of these things are."

She smiled. "Sounds like quite an adventure."

I nodded. "It was."

She told me where everything went, then as I was putting it away, she filled two glasses of water and printed a simple pasta salad, taking it all over to the table on a tray, together with two bowls and forks.

"Are you hungry?"

"Can't deny it, it's been an eventful day."

She offered me a chair and I sat down next to her.

"Try some of this."

I took a mouthful and started munching. It was a pleasant blend of tastes and textures, but there was something about it … "I can't remember ever having this before, but it's somehow familiar."

She beamed. "Back when we were first married, we used to eat this all the time. It was the quickest and cheapest thing we both really liked. I tweaked the recipe over the years, this was our favourite version."

I smiled and nodded. "Well, I still like it."

"Can you tell me about your adventure? I mean, everyone knows about the Programme, but it's hard to imagine what it must be like to go through it."

I recounted everything that happened, and all the things I learned that stood out to me (Ellie was especially pleased by my behaviour at the pool under the waterfalls).

" ... and then I found the tower and waited by the front doors until someone familiar came along, I was just about to give up and go home when you arrived."

"That would have been terrible."

"Not really, I was intending to come back again each evening until I did meet someone."

"Still, it would have been more days apart."

"So how did we first meet?"

"I worked for the Human Resources Department of Musco, and I was supposed to interview you for a design development post. I was only just back to work after my dad died a week earlier, and I wasn't handling things all that well. You were the first interview I did, you noticed I was upset and asked if there was something wrong. I told you about my dad, you asked what he was like and we got talking. I ended up crying on your shoulder for half an hour, babbling about my favourite childhood memories. You were such a good listener.

"One of the other girls from HR came into the office when it was time for the next interview, took one look at us and started laughing. I'd never been so embarrassed in all my life, but you stood up for me, telling her how I'd been through a very tough time with my dad and everything. She left the room all subdued and apologetic; I felt really valued and appreciated and was well on the way to falling head over heels in love with you."

"Wow."

"You had your interview with someone else and got hired. The boss could see I wasn't fit for work and gave me an extra week off, I gave you my number and you came to see me every day. You really cared about what I was going through, you helped me out in all sorts of little ways, and before the week was out I was utterly hooked. The whole interview incident spawned a series of popular jokes at the office, but I didn't mind, I had you. You proposed two months later, and we got married a month after that, everyone in the office came."

"So I'm a celebrity now?" I laughed. "Sounds like quite a life."

Her smile faded. "You don't remember any of it, do you?"

I put my hand on hers. "I wish I did. What did I do to throw all this away?"

"They said you stole half of Musco's pension fund, but I never believed it, I still don't."

"How do you know I didn't?"

"Because I know you. You weren't the perfect husband, I wasn't the perfect wife. You'd sometimes be distracted and forgetful, off in your own little world. You'd sometimes try to explain what you were working on and it would go right over my head, but you never lied to me. I could always tell when something was bothering you, and you'd tell me about it eventually."

"So you're convinced I was framed? By someone at the office?"

"I've got your case file in the bookshelf; we can go over the evidence and work out who—"

"Wait, slow down, can we have just one world-shattering revelation at a time, please?" I took a deep breath then exhaled slowly. "Oh, my. This is just … what am I supposed to say to that? Everything you're telling me, this whole place; it's familiar and foreign at the same time, welcoming and frightening. You, my wife, so beautiful. I mean, wow, what a day!" I burst out laughing. "It's all so insane."

She held my hand with both of hers. "I know; it's a lot, too much at once. I want to help you, as much as I can. I want to be there for you like you were for me. Anything I can do for you, just ask."

"All through the Programme they kept telling me that the person who I was is gone, dead. I didn't want to believe it, but now I'm here with you, I worry that I'm not who you think I am any more."

"But there's something of you left, enough to find me here."

"I went for a memory refresh in some cellar under a restaurant."

146

"In a rogue memory amplifier? That's very risky. People have been known to go insane with paranoia after visiting one of those places."

"Really? I should have thought of that, just the idea of getting my memory back was too much of a temptation, and this visit seemed to turn out well."

"It did, you were lucky, but you have to be very careful with things like that. Promise me you'll never go to a place like that again."

"I promise."

"All right. I'm sorry, I can be bossy sometimes. It's one of the things I realised about myself after you were gone."

"Don't apologise for that, you're right. It's a danger I was unaware of and needed telling about. Thank you."

"Oh, you're so nice to me."

"I think you're giving me a little too much credit, here."

"Too much credit? You escaped from the Gravity Ring, fought through the Wilderness Stage, re-educated yourself from scratch, risked your brain to get your memory back and then spent all of your money scouring the city to find me; if anything, I'm not giving you enough. Too often I took you for granted and didn't give you the benefit of the doubt. Now that I know these flaws I'll try to do better this time, really I will."

"This time?"

"Yes, didn't you come here to … I'm doing it again, aren't I? Taking you for granted."

"I came here not knowing what I'd find, or if I'd find anything at all. What did you think I came here for?"

She blushed and looked at the floor. "No, I was being stupid."

"Come on, you can tell me."

She winced and looked at me. "I, I thought you came here to carry on where we left off, to ask me to marry you again."

"Oh, boy. That's not even a train, that's a whole other juggernaut of thought."

"I'm sorry, I've been thinking about you this past nine months; about what I lost and the mistakes I made, hoping you'd come back, though I'd started to doubt it more and more these last few weeks. You could be infuriating at times, like when I wanted to talk and you just wanted some space to yourself, and we had our misunderstandings from time to time, but I wouldn't have swapped our marriage for the world."

I rubbed my face and sighed. "OK, right. I understand where you're coming from, as crazy as it sounds right now, but here's my perspective. When I was wandering the city, I had no idea what I was looking for. I just had a vague hope that I could rediscover who I was before the Programme, that there might be someone waiting for me, somewhere. If I said I was disappointed with who I found, it would be a terrible lie, but I hardly know you. I hardly even know who you remember me to be. Can you meet me halfway here? Let me get to know you, and who I was, and you who I am now before we make that sort of decision? I don't know if I can ever live up to that memory you have of me, if I'll ever be him again."

"I don't want you to be exactly the same as you were before, well maybe I do, but I can keep reminding myself that it's not going to happen. I can help you recover as much as possible, but if I start assuming too much, feel free to kick me."

"I don't think I could bring myself to kick you, couldn't it be something more pleasant instead?"

"Well, don't make it too pleasant, or it might not work as a deterrent ..." she said with a smile and raised an eyebrow.

"Ah, yes," I spluttered. "I didn't mean to, you know, make you—" then I noticed her giggling. "Are you making fun of me?"

"Who, me?" she leant her head to one side and fluttered her eyelashes at me, then relaxed and grinned. "You have to admit you walked right into that one."

I grinned back. "And here I thought Walker was a compliment. You want to be stuck with that name, too?"

She shrugged. "There are worse fates out there."

"I suppose there are. All right, um, as a signal that you're going too quickly, how about just a hand on your shoulder and a shake of the head? That should be clear enough, shouldn't it?"

"Yeah, that could work. OK, I'll go and get the photo albums, see if we can trigger some other memories, then I'll show you the rest of the house."

"Sounds like a plan."

"Aww, you used to say that a lot." She placed a hand on my shoulder.

"I did?"

"Mm-hm." She nodded. "That's a good sign, isn't it?"

I put my hand on hers. "Let's hope so."

She squeezed my shoulder and moved off into the next room, briefly eyeing me up and down as she went past. "Hmm, you've put on some muscle since I last saw you."

"That'll be thanks to the Wilderness Stage, though the Academy has some good sports facilities."

"Well, that's one difference I won't be complaining about. Be right back."

She brought back two large books bound in white leather with gold trim.

She opened the first page of the first book, and in the middle was a heart-shaped picture of a thinner, younger, acne-plagued version of me with unkempt hair wearing grubby green overalls, looking at the camera with a sullen expression.

On the right was a similar-shaped picture of a younger Eleanor, dressed in some sort of pristine school uniform, smiling at the camera and looking elegant and sophisticated.

Underneath the two pictures was written in gold lettering: *What did these two ever have in common?*

"That's a good question."

"Oh, that was just Jack's little joke. He had a bit of a thing for me when we were at school together, but I never thought of him as more than a friend."

149

"And you let him do our wedding album?"

"He runs a graphic art studio; he gave it to us as a wedding present. It's all very tastefully done."

The next page at the top had teenage me sitting at a battered desk surrounded by piles of engineering books alongside a picture of her reclining in an armchair with a copy of *Oliver Twist*. Below was the caption:

A love of reading,

The next pair of pictures was one of me in a slightly ill-fitting white T-shirt and shorts holding a badminton racket, and one of her leaning against a bike next to a burly young man in stylish riding gear with a fashionable hairstyle and his chest puffed out. Something about him felt off, like he was putting on an act.

Sport,

"You used to like badminton, you even represented your school once."

"By the looks of things, the entire team plus about twenty others would need to have been off sick for that to happen."

She shrugged. "Something like that. It doesn't matter, I wasn't exactly a sporting superstar either."

"Who's that next to you?"

"Oh, that's Jack. Jack Marks."

"The same one who made the book?"

"Yes, he's a friend of the family. He was always popular with the other girls at school, and used to joke about marrying me one day, but I never thought of him as more than a friend. He took me for granted all the time, got annoyed with me whenever I didn't want to do what he was doing, and was never there when I needed him. He's grown up a bit now, of course, but still not for me."

A rival for my wife's affections, that'd explain the discomfort.

On the next page was me in those same grubby overalls assembling some sort of mechanism, Eleanor in her picture was in a flowery dress and wide-brimmed straw hat weaving an ornate basket.

150

Creativity,

Below that on the left I was still in those overalls, though this time adjusting a series of half-pipes that spilt water onto a pyramid of stones in the middle of a garden pond. On the right she was in some pale blue overalls with tousled hair and dark streaks on her sleeves, legs, forehead and cheeks, planting what I assumed was a series of flower bulbs in a bed of rich dark soil.

And gardening.

"You're so beautiful in all these pictures, I especially like this one where you're not afraid to get dirty."

"Oh, you do, do you? Streaks of dirt across my face bring out my cheekbones, or something?"

"It makes you look approachable, honest, hard-working, like someone I'd like to get to know, and team up with."

She smiled and squeezed my hand. "I'd like that."

In the picture, there was a silver-haired man standing next to her with his hand on the handle of some sort of trolley loaded with odd shapes.

"Who is that, your dad?"

"Yeah, that's him, with one of his inventions. You two would have got on so well; he was always tinkering with things and improving them. He was on Musco's board of directors for a few years."

"He was?"

"Yeah, people said it was nepotism when I got hired, maybe it was when Jack got in, but he took no part in my hiring process. He told me I shouldn't even go for an interview there."

"Wait, Jack works at Musco, as well?"

"Yes, in their PR department. His studio was bought by Musco to do all of their advertising, and Jack was put in charge of it."

"With the way he talked about you, you don't think he could have …"

151

"Jack? No, he's not like that kind of guy, and he never could have made the evidence all point to you like that. I'll go and get the file, and you can see what I mean—"

"No, no, let's not deal with that now, sorry I asked. Let's concentrate on remembering who I am for now, OK?"

"All right."

The next page contained pictures of a slightly older but still thinner-looking me in a very elegant suit. I appeared nervous, and was flanked by three others who seemed to be enjoying a joke and were dressed with slightly more reserve. On my left was Jack, to my right was a man about my age, maybe a little older, with short brown hair and a hooked nose. On his right was a definitely older man with slightly sunken eyes and a receding hairline. Both of them made me feel uneasy.

"So who are these other two?"

"The one next to you is Malcolm Gray. He worked alongside you in the design development department, and the older man is Alan Stone, head of the department. After you'd been in the company for two years, Alan made you his assistant, then after your conviction Malcolm took over that position."

So, someone after my job, or my boss with some sort of dark secret? Maybe it was none of them and I did do it? No, stop it, stop thinking like that, just concentrate on rediscovering who you were.

On the opposite page, my younger self's mouth hung open and his eyes were widened in an expression of pure delight at something out of shot.

I turned the page and I'm sure that very same expression flooded my features.

The entirety of the next page was filled with a picture of Ellie in her wedding dress, with another image from another angle on the facing page. The gown's elaborately sculpted flowing fabrics enhanced her stately figure and drew attention to the radiant beauty of her face, highlighted and accentuated by subtle touches of cosmetics and gentle flowers woven into her expertly braided hair. It was an image of triumphant innocence, of glorious purity, ready and eager to offer herself to me, of all people.

I looked up from the image to Ellie, who was beaming back at me. I glanced back and forth between her and the image several times.

"You're, stunning. This is you."

"That's me." She turned the page. "This is us."

On the next page we were standing at the altar together, holding each other's hand as a priest in white and gold robes addressed the audience. I had never felt so unworthy of such an honour in my life. In the next, the priest was smiling broadly and we were both giggling. On the opposite page I was putting a ring on her finger, then she was putting one on mine.

"I gave myself to you, and you gave yourself to me. The best decision I ever made."

All around the image on the next page there were golden lightning bolts shooting out in all directions. The image was of our first kiss as man and wife.

"Wow, that's some good marketing, it looks like something out of a fairy tale."

"You want something more down to earth? Then come up and see the garden."

She stood and led me by the hand to a door at the corner of the room that opened onto a straight staircase with a wooden bannister. As soon as the door was opened, a range of earthy and floral scents swept down into the room. I looked up and saw long spiky leaves peeking over the edge of the top of the stairs, and a bright yellow luminescent ceiling above.

We walked up the stairs to an open space the size of the flat with a transparent dome in the middle, which was obviously where the 'daylight' down into the kitchen was coming from. There was also a small grassy lawn with two ponds, each roughly three metres in diameter, a couple of flower beds and multiple dark brown discs in the soil. A narrow paved path ran around the dome and past the ponds to a small patio on the other side, on which stood a simple bench and behind that a hammock hung between two tree trunks that ran from the floor to the ceiling, a height of perhaps three metres. There were several other such trunks dotted around the space, and the balustrade continued beyond the stairs as a handrail that followed the path. The wall to my left and the one on the opposite side were both a translucent pale blue, the other two walls depicted rolling fields and a distant ocean in one direction and a peaceful forest scene in the other.

"Wow. I've been saying that a lot recently, haven't I?"

"I managed to keep most of the things up here, those gaps are where statues or potted plants used to be."

"How do you get trees to grow like that? I didn't see any roots downstairs."

"Those aren't trees, it's just a wooden decoration printed onto the surface of the building's support columns. Come and see the ponds."

We walked along the path a little way, the first pond was round with rough stones around its edge, a small fountain in the middle and had various watery plants growing in it. The odd murky flash of colour could be seen in its depths.

"This one is for the fish."

The second pond was roughly the same shape and colour, but it was surrounded by neat interlocking brickwork and stairs from the path led down into the water. There was also a thin wooden disc suspended above it, perhaps two metres above the surface and two in diameter. It was engraved with a long spiral pattern and there were eight notches in its outer edge where the spiral arms ended.

"And this one is for people?"

"Yes, this water is kept warm and is very nice for a soak."

"Given the gardening pictures in the wedding album, I'm surprised there's no elaborate water feature here, or did you have to sell those, too? I'm sorry, that's really insensitive and ungrateful of me, isn't it?"

"I did sell the one in the fish pond and replaced it with that, but I couldn't bear to get rid of the one you made."

"So where is it?" I asked, looking around the brickwork for holes

"Let me show you."

She moved over to the nearest 'tree' and pressed down on a small sprouting 'twig', which flipped from pointing upwards to pointing downwards. A sound of flowing water could be heard above the disc, drips started to form along the spiral lines and then drop into the pool, after several seconds eight clear columns of water arced into the main body of water.

"That's nice, but from here you can't really see what's happening ... oh."

The drips along the lines grew more frequent then briefly turned into shifting curtains of water as the spiral arms slowly separated and warped, their edges curving up and the arms unravelling and twisting.

"You used an ancient wood printing art so that the pieces change their shape when they get wet. You worked on it for ages, then gave it to me for our fifth anniversary."

"What are they turning into?"

"Wait and see."

The water continued to stream down the arms as they morphed organically into their new shape, changing the point at which the bulk of the glistening stream spilled off an edge until each arm formed a flowing angled parabola that caught the flow and redirected it along a perfectly banked quarter-pipe and ejected it from the end of the arm in a glassy stream that pointed back towards the middle of the pool. Each arm now ended about a metre above the surface and metre from the centre, with the streams all landing together.

"You should see it at night; a different colour of light shines down each stream, and they all combine into white at the end."

"I made this? I love it, it makes the water look so inviting."

"Is this down to earth enough for you?"

"Yes, I mean, it's great, I—"

I glanced across at her. She smirked at me with dark streaks across her cheeks and forehead. I looked down at the rich dark soil in the bed next to us that she had grabbed a scoop of while I was distracted.

I chuckled. "Oh, yes, that's much better, but it's missing a little something."

I crouched down, scooped up a little soil in my fingers and dabbed a dark spot onto the tip of her beautiful nose.

"There we go, perfect."

She smiled an irresistible smile. I leant forward and kissed her. She kissed me back, then I did the same, and we held each other in a long kiss before the tornado of emotions rushing around inside me was too much and I drew my head back and exhaled.

"Wow, that fairy tale wasn't far off."

She grinned. "Does this mean—"

A sharp mechanical buzz echoed up from the dome behind us. Her eyes widened and she put both hands over her mouth. "Oh crap, it's Jack!"

Chapter 17 – An Old Friend

"Jack? Jack's here?"

"I invited him to dinner, that's what the shopping was for. Oh, this is a mess. Quick, you go and answer the door while I clean myself up and get started."

I rushed downstairs, across to the front door, then slowed down just as I was about to reach the handle.

What am I doing?

I looked back, and saw Ellie scampering over to what I assumed was her bathroom. Our eyes met, she mouthed 'it's OK', and gestured for me to continue before disappearing through the doorway. A second or two later, I heard the hiss of water rushing out of a tap.

There were two panels next to the door; one displayed a wide-angle view of the whole corridor and the one above it showed a flat view of what was in front of the door. It was definitely him; the same proud nose, bulky build, piercing blue eyes and shoulder-length dirty blond hair I'd seen in the photo album, dressed immaculately and holding a beautiful bunch of flowers.

The buzzer sounded again. I took a deep breath and opened the door.

"Hello, Ellie, you're look—" Jack's mouth hung open and his grip on the flowers slowly loosened until it fell to the floor.

I winced. "Hello, Jack."

"What the hell are you doing here?" he shouted. "You're dead."

"Not exactly, it's kind of a long story—"

Before I could continue, he grabbed me by the chest pocket of my overalls and pulled me into the corridor, slamming me into the far wall. The shock of the impact made my pulse surge.

OK, he's as strong as he looks. That's not so good.

I held up a hand. "Wait, you don't have to do this, Jack."

"Are you insane? You steal my girl, steal everyone's life savings, get off scot free and here you are stealing my girl again. You expect me to be fine with that?"

He accentuated the 'fine' by punching me hard in the stomach, which would have hurt a lot more if I hadn't been expecting it.

I ducked just under the swinging right hook he followed up with so that it only glanced off the top half of my head, though it still made my ears ring a little.

He'd let go of my pocket to take that second swing at me, so I was able to stumble back covering my head to put some distance between us, though he managed to land a slap across my mouth with the tips of his fingers as I turned, then planted a kick on my rear end to send me sprawling down the corridor. I scrambled to my feet and backed away a little further. He feigned chasing after me and I took a step back.

He laughed and shook his head. "Same old Stevie the coward, nothing's changed." He gestured towards the lift shafts. "Run along home now, and leave Ellie to me."

My mind was flooded with a faceless army of my peers howling in derision at my bumbling failure. I hung my head in shame and slunk towards the silvery doors, then stopped and shook my head. "No."

Jack raised an eyebrow. "No?"

"Everything's changed." I drew myself up to my full height and the vision faded. "I'm not who you think I am. My name is Zephyr Walker."

He laughed again. "Zephyr? What kind of stupid name is that?"

"Zephyr that I came from a place full of wind and fury, signifying nothing. Walker that I did not consider equality with nothingness something to cling to, but made myself something; taking on the form of an adventurer, warrior, builder, philosopher; engineer, servant of the weak and frail, follower of the good at which all things aim, and now defender of my beloved." I took up a fighting stance. "I have persevered through disorientation and weakness, betrayal and toil, temptation and near death. I will not give in to complacency or fear, I will not allow bullies like you to take whatever you want without a fight."

159

"Why you arrogant little piece of filth. Now you're going to get it."

He charged at me, swinging another big right hook at my head. I moved forward and down inside the blow, deflecting his punch with my left wrist, then in one movement rose up again, thrusting the heel of my right hand hard up into his nose, then disengaging as he brought his hands up to cover his face.

"Argh! You revolting freak! You're going to pay for that."

"Just stop now, Jack."

He wiped the tears streaming from his eyes and blinked with his hands waving in front of his face, then decided he knew where I was and went for me again, swinging wildly. I ducked under the blow and got around behind him, grabbing a handful of his long hair and pulling his head back as far as it would go, placing a foot behind his knee and forcing him down onto his knees with my fist at his throat.

"Are you going to stop now, or do I have to hurt you?"

He started to struggle, landed an elbow in my ribs, then just as I brought my hand back to carry out my threat, we both heard a faint mechanical humming noise. We looked up to see Ellie pointing what looked like some sort of gun at Jack's head.

"That's enough, Jack. I was not, am not and never will be your girl. Right now, you just lost me as a friend. You go now, and don't come back."

I now wasn't sure whether the tears in his eyes were from the blow to his nose or from Ellie's pronouncement.

"Ellie, please, don't," he whimpered. "He's a trickster, a thief, and a con man. Can't you see what he's doing to you, to both of us, again? You can't believe him."

"I said that's enough, Jack. Are you going to go now, or do I have to use this? You know I won't miss."

"I'm going, I'm going." He relaxed, and after a couple of seconds I released his hair. He stood and walked slowly to the lift shaft with drooped shoulders. Ellie's weapon remained trained on

160

him until he was at the doors. She lowered her gun as he pressed the button to call for a lift, but both of us watched him intently.

He sighed as the hum of the shaft heralded an approaching cabin. "Think about what you're doing. Don't rush into anything you'll regret later, please?"

She raised an eyebrow. "Like you just did?"

His head dropped and he sighed again. "Yeah."

The doors opened. "Bye, Ellie."

"Goodbye, Jack."

He stepped through the doors, they closed and the cabin was whisked down to the ground floor.

Ellie slumped against the wall of the corridor and sighed. "I'm sorry, I had no idea he would do that."

"It's all right, how are you supposed to know what someone else will do? You can't read … minds. Oh."

"What is it?"

"An unpleasant thought. Jack seemed to be pretty convinced that I did the crime."

"Of course he would be, the evidence pointed to you, but—"

"If you were wrong about what Jack would do, could you be just as wrong about me?"

"Oh, great. That is really not a helpful thought right now."

"I mean, I can't imagine ever wanting to do that crime, the very thought of someone doing it makes me sick, but I'm not who I was before the Programme. I don't know what I was thinking."

She sighed and looked away. "This is … a lot. A lot to think about."

"Should I give you some space? Come back another day?"

He voice went very quiet. "Do you want to go?"

I could see the tension in her shoulders, but what did it mean? What did she want me to say? *How about the truth?*

"No."

"Then what do you want?"

I put my hand on her shoulder. "I want to help you. If you need some space, I'll let you have it, but I'd like to get to know you again. I want to find out as much as I can about who I was, then combine the best of me then with the best of me now. I'd like to rekindle this great marriage you keep talking about, introduce you to the people I've met, and go on a great adventure together."

She put her hand on mine, and there was a big smile in her voice. "Sounds like a plan." She turned to face me. "I'd say it's been quite an adventure already today."

"Can't argue with that."

She then lifted her chin and put on her haughtiest expression. "Brave Sir Walker, you have defended our honour, what can we do to express our gratitude?"

I went down on one knee and kissed her hand. "Oh, my lady! Your beauty surpasses all the heavens. My one great wish is for your hand in marriage."

She lifted both hands above her head with an enormous grin. "Yay!"

I stood and wrapped my arms around her, she wrapped hers around me, and we held each other for a long time.

"Thank you for waiting for me."

"Thank you for finding me."

"Right now I don't care whether the previous me did it or not. If I did, I paid the price for it; it's over, it's done. If I didn't and someone framed me, I forgive them. I have you, we have this place and all these possibilities. I'm home."

Chapter 18 – Cleaning Up

She squeezed me tighter and I felt a twinge of pain in my ribs. "Ow."

"You're hurt."

"Oh, it's, he just hit quite hard. Yeah, I'll give him that. I'll recover."

"I've got something for that inside. Come on."

She retrieved a small can of something from her bathroom cupboard and told me to spray it on my injuries. It didn't seem to do anything immediately, but over the next few minutes the pain became less and less noticeable.

"So how long would it take to get remarried?"

"That would depend on how big an event you want to make it. If you don't want to invite anyone or do anything fancy, then we could get it done by noon tomorrow. If we wanted to invite our mums, then it might take a couple of weeks to arrange things, or months if you wanted to make a big event out of it."

"Our mums? They're both alive?"

"Yeah, but they live a long way away and don't get on that well. It was quite a struggle to get them to be civil to each other at the first wedding. Don't get me wrong, I like your mum, but there's something about you and her that sets my mum on edge, I don't know what it is. It'll take a few days to get in contact with your mum, she likes being far away from civilisation."

"I thought I was like your dad."

"Yeah, that might be it – she often got very annoyed with him, too. She always told me I shouldn't make the same mistake as her and marry beneath my station. Apparently we're distant descendants of some noble family line back on Earth. Not that anything like that has ever mattered out here. I love her dearly, but she's difficult sometimes."

"Hmm, that's a shame."

There was an awkward pause.

"So, do you think we could look at the evidence against me? I mean, the old me?"

"I thought you didn't care whether you did it?"

"It's more of a nagging curiosity, an intellectual itch I need to scratch. It's part of knowing who I was."

"All right." She went and got a file of papers that included security logs from the building, data logs from Musco's internal network and account information from a number of banks. She spread it out on the kitchen table and summarised it for me.

"All the building's security recordings were knocked out for half an hour. During that time someone hacked into the company's budget allocation system from the work terminal in your office and planted a virus. Each time an acquisition was made for raw materials or spare parts, the virus transferred four per cent of the amount to an external account as a 'broker's commission', and sent a matching amount to the acquisitions fund from the company's pension scheme to mask the transfer. The broker account had been set up a week earlier from your terminal during another security blackout.

"Nobody in the office remembered anything out of the ordinary during those times, and everyone in the office was in pretty much the same place at the start and end of both blackouts, you being in your office both times. There were no other fingerprints or biotraces on your console, no anomalous keystroke profiles, and access codes for the account were uploaded to your holoband from your terminal during the second blackout."

"That all looks pretty damning. You think someone could have falsified the records so it looked like it was being done from my terminal?"

"I don't know, it's not my field, but I suppose it's possible. I think they considered that during the investigation."

"Then what makes you so sure I didn't do it?"

"Like I said, it seemed so unlike you. I knew you better than anyone, am I not allowed a little faith in my husband?"

"Of course, but after yesterday and what you've shown me today, I'm prepared to concede that I did the crime, paid for it and move on."

She hung her head and sighed. "So am I."

A wave of fatigue swept over me. "What a day."

"We won't forget this one in a hurry."

I helped to put the papers back in the file, then picked up a chair and took her hand, leading her to the sofa. I put the chair next to the end of the sofa and invited her to sit down "I'll be back in a minute."

"What are you going to do?"

"You'll see."

I went to the kitchen unit and printed another bowl of the pasta salad and then a small flower from the 4-D printer, and filled two plastic cups with water. I carried it back to her on the same tray she had used before. As I approached, I saw that she had buckled her holoband to the back of the chair and was using it to project the image of a cheerily burning fire in a hearth onto a blank section of wall in front of the sofa.

"Sorry, it's all I can afford right now."

"It's fine, it's perfect."

I put the tray down on the chair, handed her a cup of water and the flower then sat down next to her. She sniffed the flower and smiled at me.

"Aww, you shouldn't have."

"It's not as if it costs me anything."

She took a sip from the cup, handed it back to me and snuggled up to me, gazing at the flower. I put my arms around her, cupping her flower-holding hand in mine.

"This is a good way to end the day."

"Mmm," she purred, her breathing slowed and steadied, and soon she was fast asleep. She just fit in my arms so naturally, her chest slowly rising and falling, so warm, so peaceful, so safe. It wasn't long until my own head started drooping and before I knew it I was dreaming of floating over fields and mountains, beyond worlds and stars.

166

The daylight pouring down from the garden floor caught the corner of my eye as I opened them, the stiffness in my neck was obvious as soon as I tried to move.

"Ow."

Ellie's eyes flicked open, she looked up at me and smiled. She had slept the whole night in my arms. "Good morning." She sighed happily, then narrowed her eyes and pouted slightly as if scolding me for my impertinence. "You're here. It wasn't a dream."

"No, it wasn't." I smiled, then grimaced as I rolled my neck from side to side and massaged it with my free hand.

She yawned, sat up and stretched with various groans, then held up an index finger. "I vote next time we do this in the other room, the one designed for sleeping in."

"Sounds like a plan. What were you going to do today?"

"Whatever I had in mind is long since out of the window and smashed to pieces on the pavement below."

I glanced across at the chair. "There's some pasta salad left for breakfast, let's share it and decide on something together."

She stood up straight and saluted. "Right you are, Cap'n!"

We munched on the salad, she added some fresh rolls and juice from the previous day's shopping, and we discussed the various arrangements we'd need to make to get remarried. Just as I was washing the dishes, the door buzzer went.

Ellie looked up. "Who could that be?"

"You're not expecting anyone?"

"No." She moved towards the door.

"It'd better not be Jack again."

She looked at the screen and appeared taken aback. "No, it's not. You should come and see this."

I opened the door with Ellie beside me, and there was Alan Stone and Malcolm Gray. Mr Stone appeared stern and businesslike, Mr Gray was slowly shaking his head and sighing as if he couldn't believe this was happening.

"Hello, Steven."

"Hello, Mr Stone and Mr Gray?"

167

"So you remember our names," Malcolm said with an accusatory glare.

"I saw your pictures in the wedding album, Ellie told me your names."

"We were told that there was a vanishingly small chance of coming across you again, and even if we did, you would have no memories of us or your previous life."

Should I admit what I did to refresh my memory?

"I don't really remember anything, just the faintest impressions."

Malcolm's brow furrowed. "And yet this was enough to find your wife again and carry on as if nothing happened, making a mockery of the whole process?"

"I had to know who I was. I would have kept going for as long as it took to find someone who knew me."

"Still inquisitive and tenacious, I see," Alan commented. "That hasn't changed."

"You are going to praise him for flouting the law?"

"Calm down, Malcolm, the law is on his side right now, much as it is inconvenient for us. Legally he is a different person, and the price has been paid for his crime. The only issue as far as the law is concerned is Mr Marks' unprovoked assault on Mr ...?"

"Walker. Zephyr Walker"

"As you can see, Mr Walker, according to the law you are a different person, but many of us in the company won't see it that way. A lot of people felt betrayed. A lot of people were very angry with you, and clearly still are. I think it would be best if you avoid any contact with the company's staff from now on, I will ensure that they stay away from you. Do you intend to press charges against Mr Marks?"

"I do not. I understand his frustrations and will keep my distance from him as much as possible."

"That is very gentlemanly of you, thank you. What are your intentions from here on?"

"I'm starting out as a maintenance technician for 4-D printers. Ellie and I were going to get married, again, if that's the right word."

"Miss Charter, are you sure that is wise, considering all that has happened?"

"It is a mutual decision, and one I am very happy with," she replied, squeezing my hand, and I felt a surge of pride.

"Ordinarily I would congratulate you both, but this makes for a very awkward situation, since Miss Charter was applying to rejoin the company. Should you marry him again, Miss Charter, there may well be another backlash against you, or at least a significant poisoning of the company atmosphere once word gets out about Mr Charter's, I mean Mr Walker's return. It saddens me to say it, but if you cannot be dissuaded from this path, I think it would be best if we terminate your probation period before it begins and you also agree to keep your distance from Musco employees."

Ellie sighed and bowed her head.

I turned to her. "You don't have to do that for me, I—"

She held up a hand and shook her head to silence me.

"I understand that this is a difficult choice. You were a fine employee and we would, of course, provide you with the best of references to a future employer, but please reconsider. I will tell everyone at the company that a family issue has come up and you will need a week to deal with it. We will be back here at the end of that week to hear your decision. Shall we say nine in the morning on Saturday?

"Um, yes, that should be fine."

"Then we are agreed. Good day to you both."

"Goodbye, Mr Stone, Mr Gray."

"Goodbye, Mr Walker," Malcolm said with a note of finality.

Alan sighed in disappointment. "A most regrettable situation. Goodbye, Mr Walker."

I put my arms around Ellie in the doorway and quietly held her. I was just able to make out their conversation as they moved down the corridor to the lift shaft.

"I was half-expecting you to offer him his old job back. He was always your favourite."

"Don't be ridiculous, Malcolm."

"Why was that? He hardly ever contributed anything to our brainstorming sessions."

"And yet they are noticeably less productive since he left, aren't they? I'd say you underestimated his influence."

"And now we won't get another good employee back because of him? What a mess."

"Yes, it is. But we have to make the best of it. Onwards and upwards."

The two of them stepped into the lift shaft and the doors closed.

"I'm really sorry, Ellie, to put you through all this."

"It's just a job. Don't get me wrong, it was a really good job, and I was looking forward to going back, but some things are more important."

"So, you lost your job there when I was convicted?"

She nodded. "I applied for a position at the Academy's work placement office, so I'd have a chance of catching you on your way through the Programme, but the Academy doesn't allow it for precisely that reason. I found work at a regional employment office, which is rewarding in its own way, but I missed all my friends at Musco. I'd started to lose hope that you'd ever come back, and Jack put in a good word in for me at the company, that I'd put it all behind me."

"Hence the dinner."

She hung her head. "Yes. I'm sorry, I'd been told over and over that there was very little chance of ever seeing you again, and that I should let it go. It wears you down after a while; I'm not as strong as I thought I was."

I put a hand on her shoulder. "It's all right, I understand. I'd basically lost all hope of recovering anything from my old life until I got that offer of a memory refresh, and I considered ignoring the offer and moving on. In the end I took the offer, and eventually

170

found my way here. I'm sure there's a lot of hard work ahead, but also a lot to look forward to. If we can cultivate a marriage that's half as good as what you've been describing, then it will all have been worth it, won't it?"

She looked up at me with both hope and tears in her eyes, then wrapped her arms around me. "It will."

Two evenings later, our door buzzer went. I went to answer it, and it was Alan Stone again. I called Ellie over and opened the door.

"Hello, Mr Stone. We weren't expecting you until Saturday."

"I just wanted to check, has anyone else from the company been pestering you?

Ellie shook her head. "No, no trouble at all. You didn't come all this way just to ask that, did you?"

"No. I couldn't say this in front of Malcolm, and he and the others will call me a sentimental old fool, but I wanted to say goodbye to my friends properly."

"You know I'm not going back?"

"Yes, I could see straight away there was no way you'd change your mind, you're not that sort of girl. I'd have given you a week of paid leave if I could, but there'd be no way I could justify it to the company. I do have a wedding present for you both, though." He glanced down to the leather briefcase in his left hand.

"Do come in."

"Thank you."

He placed the briefcase on the kitchen table and opened it, retrieving two bottles of wine, a beautiful crystal decanter and six exquisite crystal glasses.

Ellie admired the glasses. "Oh, Alan, you shouldn't have."

"Don't try and talk me out of it, you know how stubborn I can be."

"All right, but they are beautiful, and you are a softie." She kissed him on the top of his head.

"There you go, I'm all paid in full." He smiled.

Ellie laughed and put three of the glasses and one of the bottles away, then opened the other and poured a drink for each of us as we sat around the table.

Alan took a sip, smiled and leant forward. "So how have you been getting on? What was it like in the Programme?"

We told him about all that we were planning, and I recounted my experiences in the programme. By the end, he was misty-eyed.

"Are you all right?" I asked.

"It's just, good to see you again. You were a good friend to me, and a fine engineer. It's so sad that all of this had to happen, and that we have to say goodbye like this."

Ellie placed a hand on his shoulder. "Do we have to say goodbye? Couldn't we remain friends?"

"You are too kind, but it would reflect badly on the company if I were known to stay in contact with you after all of this. It would be best if no one else knew I was here today."

Ellie sighed. "I understand."

"I knew you would. Well, I should be off." He stood from his chair, but grimaced and flexed the fingers of his right hand as he pushed off the armrests.

"What's the matter, Alan?" Ellie asked with genuine concern, turning to disappointment. "Oh, you haven't. You put it off again?"

Alan protected his hand and looked sheepish. "I thought I could manage it, that it still had a chance to get better."

"Put what off? What's not better?"

"Alan has a degenerative nerve condition in his right hand, that's slowly spreading up his arm. Every time the doctors think they've cured it, it comes back again. He's been scheduled for a hand replacement three times now."

"Look, I know it'll take the spasms and the weakness away, and the artificial hand will work just as well, if not better in every respect than a normal hand, but it won't be me, you know? To cut off a part of me that feels fine a lot of the time and replace it with a machine … it just seems, *unnatural*." He shivered. "They even gave me a demonstration model so I could practice doing everyday tasks with the mental interface and get used to the idea. It works really well, but it just feels so weird, so I keep putting the whole thing off, hoping the problem will go away. I know I'm not being reasonable, but you understand, don't you?"

"Yeah, I do," I said. "It's a difficult decision. Not your only one recently."

"Thank you." He picked up the briefcase. "Then all that remains is to wish you all the best together. Give my fondest regards to your mothers, and give them lots of beautiful grandchildren to spoil and enjoy."

I held Ellie closer and smiled. "That's the current plan."

"Maybe we can catch up again someday when all of this has calmed down."

Ellie nodded. "We'd like that. Should I give you a notice of resignation now? I have one ready in the other room."

"No, no, people would wonder how I got it. All of that should wait until Saturday morning, in front of everyone, the notary will have something for you to sign."

"Everyone?"

"Jack will be coming to apologize and ask you to officially drop the charges. Malcolm and I will be there to accept your withdrawal from the probation period and for us all to sign an agreement to keep our distance from each other, or not, but we know what's going to happen there. There'll be a notary present to make sure everything is above board and legally binding. Malcolm doesn't trust me to take care of this by myself; he thinks I'll get too sentimental to go through with it. He's right, of course."

I smiled and shook Alan's hand. "Thank you, Alan. It has been very nice meeting you, I wish I could remember more of our previous friendship. I look forward to catching up with you again when everything has calmed down."

Ellie gave Alan a hug and a kiss on his cheek, then stepped back to my side and took my hand. "Thanks for understanding, Alan. Take care of yourself."

"I will."

And with that, he departed and closed the door behind him.

I turned to Ellie and put my arms around her. "So, what do you say we get married on Monday?"

"The thirty-fifth of February? You want our wedding anniversary to be every seventeen years?"

"Well, it'd be fun, and wouldn't get in the way of celebrating our original anniversary, which is when?"

"Thirty-third of August. I'd be offended you've forgotten it, if you didn't have a much better excuse than most husbands. I'd prefer to have two each year, though. The thirty-third would make them perfectly spaced out, too."

"Wouldn't that be a bit hectic to have the meeting with Alan, Jack, Malcolm and the notary in the morning, then the wedding in the afternoon?"

"It'll just be a formality – five or ten minutes at most."

"Have any of our recent meetings with them gone as smoothly as you hoped?"

"Well, no …"

"I'd prefer not to risk it, and have just one set of more pleasant worries on our minds when we retie our knot."

"So, you really want the thirty-fifth?"

"With the Leap Year celebrations, it'll be like the whole planet is celebrating our wedding day."

"There is that …"

"Is that a yes?"

"All right, let's go for that. It'll be a crowded day though, with lots of people choosing that date for the same reasons. I'll contact the priest who married us the first time, and see if he can squeeze us in at some point. There are a couple of other people I can get in touch with if he can't."

"Still nothing from my mum?"

"Like I said, she only responds to handwritten paper letters, it should have arrived by now, and we'll hear back from her in a day or two."

"How will you tell her in time of our wedding date if it takes that long?"

"Here's where I get a little sneaky. I exchange letters with your mum on a regular basis. Your mum's village is very small, we visited her a few times, and I'm one of the few people that sends paper letters anymore, so I got to be friends with the postman in her village. When I'm in a hurry to contact her, I write and scan my letter, then he 3D-prints an exact copy of the letter and envelope and takes it to her door within a couple of hours. I don't think she's ever noticed the difference."

"So I have a sneaky wife, that's good to know."

"And you like that in a wife?"

"As long as you only use your powers for good."

She shrugged. "Well, mostly." Then gave me a wicked grin.

I shrugged. "Well, good enough." I grinned back. "It's good to be kept on your toes every so often."

Chapter 19 – Catharsis

The day came and Alan, Malcolm, Jack and the notary arrived. They stepped through to the kitchen and the notary placed his black leather briefcase on the table, retrieving several pieces of paper and a black pen with gold trimmings. Malcolm stood on one side of the notary, and Jack on the other, while Alan stayed back by the front door of the flat.

"I don't want to get in the way of what you all need to do. Jack, if you would like to begin."

"Yes, sir. Mr Norton, would you read out my statement, please."

"Certainly, Mr Marks." Mr Norton picked up the top document and read in a formal tone, " 'I, Jackson Phillip Marks declare that my behaviour eight days ago was irresponsible, inappropriate, unacceptable and entirely unprovoked. Mr Walker bears no responsibility for the previous existence and activities of Mr Charter, and I was entirely wrong to associate them and take such perceived revenge, which was uncalled for even if such an association did exist. I apologise unreservedly, and submit to whatever reparations Mr Walker requires of me.' "

"Thank you, Mr Norton. These are my own words, spoken of my own free will without compulsion, and I now sign this document in the presence of all of you as witnesses to attest to this fact."

Jack took the pen and signed his name at the bottom of the sheet of paper, then gave it to Mr Norton, who also signed. Jack stood stiffly by the table with his eyes closed, visible tension in his shoulders.

Mr Norton looked at me. "Mr Walker, do you wish to respond to Mr Marks' statement?"

I nodded to Mr Norton then looked at Jack. "I do. Mr Marks, I accept your apology and here before all present declare that I will not be pressing any charges against you. I am prepared to put that in writing, if required."

Jack opened his eyes and nodded at me in formal gratitude. Mr Norton also nodded. "Thank you, Mr Walker, that would be appreciated. There is room here at the bottom of Mr Marks' declaration."

I stepped over and wrote on the left side of the bottom of the page: *I accept the above apology and will not be pressing charges. Zephyr Walker.*

Mr Norton signed his own name beside mine as a witness.

I looked up at Jack. "By the way, Jack, that was a good left jab you got me with, very solid." That cracked his stern demeanour and brought a small smile to his face. "Do you think our next fight could be alongside, instead of against each other?"

Jack's smile broadened and he briefly shadow boxed. "It's a possibility."

"Ellie, would you mind if Jack came to our wedding?

"If he can behave himself . . ."

"Who, me?" Jack asked, feigning innocence, and most of the tension in the room dissipated.

"I take it the wedding is still going ahead, then?" Alan asked.

"Yes, on the thirty-fifth."

"Of course, a leap-year wedding." Alan nodded. Malcolm rolled his eyes and shook his head.

"That brings us to the second part of these proceedings," said Mr Norton. "That of Miss Charter's probationary period at Musco and future dealings with its employees. Miss Charter, please be aware that you are under no legal obligation to withdraw from your probation or to enter into this mutual restraining order, any such act will be entirely voluntary. I have here letters of reference for your future employer should you sign. Do you still wish to do so?"

Ellie nodded. "I do. I will not be changing my mind."

Alan stepped away from the door. "Before we proceed, there's something I should say."

Malcolm scowled. "What is it now, Alan? Are you going to argue against your own proposal? You said yourself that the whole company atmosphere will suffer because of Mr Charter's crime."

"It is relevant to that." Alan took a deep breath and muttered to himself, "How many times is it now?"

"How many times is what?"

Alan took a metal sphere about the size of his fist from his pocket, looked at it and shook his head. "So much trouble from a little thing like this."

"What is that?" I asked.

"This is how I got to be the Head of Design Development at Musco."

"What are you talking about?" Malcom asked. "I've never seen that thing before."

"Oh, you have, Malcolm, plenty of times."

"No I haven't, I'd have remembered—"

Alan didn't let him finish "Stevie, I mean Zephyr, do you know what you did in the company you worked for before joining Musco?"

"Ellie said I worked in IT before switching to design development, like you did in Musco."

"Yes, like I did in Musco. That really struck me about you, that you actually lived out my fantasy."

"What fantasy?"

"That someone with a background in IT could become a great inventor and solve engineering problems in the real world."

"What are you talking about, Alan?" Malcolm interjected. "You did that far more than he did, you solved more problems and had more great ideas than anyone else in the team. That's why you were made head of the department."

"But they weren't my ideas. While Stevie was working with us, most of them were his."

"No they weren't, he hardly ever said anything in the brainstorming sessions."

"No, he's a quiet man. He'd watch and listen to us discussing the problem, taking it all in, then come up with a solution that hadn't occurred to any of us. It was perfect."

"OK, that happened once or twice, I'll admit, but—"

"And that's when I'd steal them, like all the other ideas you thought were mine, with this." He held up the ball again.

"What? What is that?"

"It destabilises recent connections in the limbic system and disrupts the consolidation of new ones."

Malcolm shook his head. "I have no idea what you're talking about, Alan."

But I did. "A memory wiper."

"Yes, Stevie. When I press this button, everyone's memory of the previous five minutes are lost, and whatever they experience in the two minutes after never makes it to their long-term memory. Whenever you solved one of our problems, I'd ask you to clarify, then wipe everyone's memories and present it as my own idea. You assumed that we thought alike and I was just beating you to the punch. My whole career at Musco was a lie."

"Your whole career? But you were at Musco for a decade before he arrived."

"I stole from a wide range of people before Stevie came. He was too good at problem solving. That's why I had to frame him."

"Frame him? *You* stole the pension funds?" Jack stepped away from the table and started towards Alan.

"Stop right there, all of you!" Alan raised the metal ball over his head with his trembling right hand. "Anyone comes closer and I'll wipe your memories. I've done it before, and you'll be none the wiser. Stay where you are and let me finish this."

Jack lowered his hands. "All right, take it easy."

"Everyone sit at the table, and no sudden moves." His voice now had a slight tremble to it as well. We sat down and he stepped back towards the front door, keeping us all in the middle of his vision as he leant against the wall. "As I was saying, he was too good; he

179

came up with the solution too many times, more than anyone else in the team. Before Stevie came along, I could steal ideas from Malcolm, from Bill, from Greg, all over the place, there didn't have to be a pattern to it for people to pick up on. I couldn't stop, I needed to be the guy with the most initial ideas, I had nothing else to offer the company, other than being able to get people talking.

"I couldn't stand being the nameless IT guy that everyone ignored; people looked up to me for the first time in my life. When Stevie came along he threatened my dominance, so I had to steal from him again and again, and he started to notice. He came and told me how he was getting all discouraged, how he could never seem to speak up soon enough. I encouraged him to keep going and let him have his next few ideas, but he was getting too close to me."

The tremor in his right hand started to increase, and he reached up and steadied it with his left hand.

"You know why my hand shakes? I went to the doctor about it once. Nerve degeneration caused by repeated exposure to resonant radiation. I wear a hair piece with an integrated mesh that shields my brain from the memory wipe, but it does nothing to protect the hand that presses the button. My hand is messed up from using this damn thing too many times. I never went to a doctor about it again; I looked up whatever incurable nerve disease would give similar symptoms and forged a doctor's report that said I had it. That's how I got hold of the prosthetic hand, which I used to hack into the security system and the financial system from Stevie's terminal with no incriminating fingerprints, biotraces or keystroke style to lead back to me. I did it with him in the room, even showed him how the hand worked and let him try it out so it would learn his keystroke profile, then I wiped his memory, and the memories of all those who saw me going into and out of his office.

"It had to be something heinous to get him thrown in the Programme. Destroying the livelihoods of those who had improved the lives of those around them for decades and had earned their rest was as bad as I could do in a way that would trace back to him. I saw it as self-defence, and I tried to ensure it would be discovered before too much damage was done, it was all cold calculation. It worked as well as I could hope: the money was recovered, the threat to my position was removed, and no one suspected me.

"It was only after he was gone that what I'd done hit me. I'd destroyed an honest hard-working employee who did nothing wrong; he was just too good at his job. What really broke me was the effect it had on Ellie. She was fined double what couldn't be recovered and fired from her position in the company. I called for civility, but on her way out she received torrents of abuse from the other employees. She endured it all with her head held high."

What can I do from here to stop him? As soon as I stand from my chair or make any sudden moves, he'll push the button.

"I went to visit her and check on how she was doing, found she was struggling to get a new job and keep up payments on the flat, her reputation in ruins for something she never did, and not even her husband did. I told her to give potential new employers my name so I could give her as positive a reference as possible, which I hope helped her land her current job. I even confessed my guilt to her a couple of times before wiping her memory, but my guilt never went away, it wasn't enough."

I glanced at the table, there was just the decanter and glasses on it. *I could throw one of those at him to distract him, but he'd see me reaching across the table for it. There has to be something else ...*

Alan looked me in the eye. "I hired a private investigator to watch out for your exit from the Programme, and follow you, to make sure you would be offered a memory refresh and hopefully find your way back to Ellie. If that hadn't worked, I would have told him to plant clues to Ellie's whereabouts near your flat. I already knew about Jack's fight with you before he called to tell us about it. When I came back here last week I confessed again, to both of you, but I couldn't go through with it, couldn't give up all the prestige and wealth I'd stolen, so I wiped your memories again. Maybe today, in front of all of you, I'll be stronger."

I took hold of Ellie's hand under the table and felt the crystal stopper from the decanter that she was holding. I gently prised it from her hand and transferred it to my stronger right hand. I felt the weight of it and my mind flashed back to the rock-throwing training I had with the Apples. *If I can hit the memory wiper, maybe I can damage it or knock it out of his hand, then get to it before he can.* It would be a difficult throw, but Ellie sitting next to me would shield my intentions from him until it was too late. I gripped the front corner of my chair with my left hand, tensed my leg muscles ready to pounce, pointed my left shoulder slightly to his left and slowly lowered my right hand ready to throw. *I must have tried something last time. I hope it wasn't this ...*

The trembling in Alan's right hand grew more pronounced, and there was now also a trembling in his voice as he shook his head. "I'm not strong. I can't do it, I'm so sorry ..."

I flung the stopper at the metal sphere, just missing to the left and cracking into the wall behind him as I pushed my chair back and charged towards him.

Alan ducked and flinched away from the flying projectile, his right hand spasmed and the memory wiper slipped from his grasp. His eyes opened wide as he saw it fall; he snatched down at it, but only succeeded in accelerating it towards the floor where it landed with a crunch on the hard tiles, shedding small pieces in several directions.

He sank to his knees as I arrived and kicked the main piece out of his reach, then stood over him. "A week ago I told Ellie that if I'd been framed, I forgave whoever did it. That still stands, but I have to put a stop to this."

Tears welled up in his eyes as he gazed at the little spread of wreckage. "It's gone. I'm finished." He started to sob and collapsed to the floor, then those sobs turned into laughter as he rolled onto his back and looked up at me. "It's over. I'm finally going to pay for what I did. Thank you, Stevie. You're a good man."

Malcolm shook his head. "Wait, let me get this straight. Stevie didn't do any of the things he was thrown into the Programme and out of the company for? That was all you?"

"Yes, it was all me, Malcolm. Neither of them did anything wrong."

"You realise that you'll get thrown into the Programme for this?"

"And it will be well earned. No one will have deserved it more. I look forward to it, it'll be a relief to shed this despicable life and start again. Maybe they'll finally fix my hand before dropping me into the Gravity Ring."

Mr Norton rose from his chair. "I will call the authorities. Besides the clearly illegal acts committed with that device, I'm fairly certain even possession of such a thing is against the law, or soon will be. They will be highly interested in how you obtained it."

"Of course I'll cooperate fully with any investigation, and do all I can to help catch the lowlifes that sold me that infernal thing. I have nothing to lose now, I can only hope to help as much as possible before being wiped. Mr Norton, would it be too late to write a last will and testament before the authorities arrive? I wish for half of all that I possess after the law takes what is required to be left to the children of my estranged wife, and half to Miss Charter and Mr Walker, in addition to whatever the law awards them. Would that be possible?"

"It would, if we are quick about it."

Malcolm turned to me. "I'm sorry, Mr Walker. I had no idea, about any of this. I still don't know what to make of all of these revelations, or how everyone else at the company will react."

"Don't worry, Mr Gray. We won't be insisting on our positions at Musco being returned. We are both gainfully employed, with exciting opportunities on the horizon. Besides, I'm not properly trained for my old post any more."

I contacted Bern and Gram, who had married Helen in the meantime, and we started making plans for Sidereos Settlements Incorporated. Ellie put us in touch with several capable people via her employment office, and Mr Norton advised us on legal matters.

At our request, Alan was permitted a temporary release from custody to attend our wedding, though he was fitted with a tracking device and accompanied by a pair of plain-clothes police officers. Everyone in Sidereos Settlements was there, together with Pat, Jack and my mum. Ellie was unable to convince her mum to come at such short notice, though I suspect she may have had other reasons for not attending.

After the ceremony, we went outside to watch the whole planet celebrate our wedding day with fireworks, streamers, street performances and liquid ballets. Some of them might have been celebrating other weddings or the leap year, but we didn't mind. The day after carrying her over the threshold, I piled some extra soil on top of the deepest bed in the garden floor and planted my disparity tree seed.

"I hope you like your new home, Mr Tree, I know I do."

Alan's cooperation with the investigation proved helpful, leading to the arrest of the men who sold him the memory wiper and many of their associates, though some remained elusive. We attended Alan's private hearing, where he did not contest any of the charges, pleading guilty on all counts, and requesting that his subsequent cooperation with the authorities not be taken into account. The judge's verdict was clear, he was to be thrown into the Programme and we were awarded four times Ellie's previous fine.

Alan was taken through to the memory chamber, where he was sat restrained in a reclining chair. On the other side of the armoured glass stood Ellie and I.

"Well, this is it, Alan."

"Yes, it is, Zeph, Ellie. Is everyone well?"

"Very, your resources will really help to get things going, meaning we can build our own interplanetary transports instead of hiring them. We've got our drones, printer and power plant all tested and ready; we have our parcels of land on Sidereos picked out and if things continue to go well, should be deploying at our first site next week. In other news," – I held Ellie closer and smiled – "don't tell anyone, but we're off to the doctor this afternoon. We think Ellie might be expecting."

Alan smiled. "That's great news! Congratulations! I think we can safely say your secret's safe with me."

"Who knows, maybe we'll catch you on the other side."

"Now there's a nice thought to go under with."

"I'm afraid I'm going to have to hurry you, sir," said the guard standing next to Alan as he pressed a button and silvery panels began to swing down from the ceiling to enclose the chair.

"Wait, will he remember anything we tell him now?" I urgently asked the guard, as I could see Alan was struggling to keep his eyes open.

"It's unlikely, but you never know."

I thumped my fist against the glass and called out, "You're not flying, you're falling. Catch yourself."

END OF BOOK 1
TO BE CONTINUED IN BOOK 2: *SIDEREOS, INC.*

About the Author

Ben Zwycky is an English ex-pat now living in the Czech Republic. Before, during and after obtaining a master's degree in chemical engineering, he worked as a hospital porter, research assistant, cleaner and server in a Salvation Army community centre, EFL teacher and currently works as a freelance proofreader and translator together with his Czech wife, who literally fell into his arms in the year 2000 and with whom he now has five children.

Beyond the Mist is his second novel. His debut, *Nobility Among Us*, is available on Kindle and in Paperback, as is his first poetry collection, *Selected Verse – Faith and Family*.

He is a contributing editor to *Sci Phi Journal* and a regular contributor to superversiveSF.com. You can find out more about him and his work at www.benzwycky.com.

51044010R00103

Made in the USA
Charleston, SC
13 January 2016